Apache Kid

Apache Kid

Historical Fiction

A Short Novel

By

W. H. Short

This is a work of fiction. Names, characters and incidents are either the product of the authors imagination or used fictitiously. Several actual historical personalities are used, however, there is no evidence any such incidents such as described in this novel ever occurred. Any other resemblance to actual persons, either living or dead are entirely coincidental. However, all of the chapter introductions are facts.

Other books by this Author:

Two Weeks
High Ground
Diving Dictionary

DEDICATION

To my Wife of 45 years
Lorraine Eva Short

ACKNOWLEDGMENTS

My thanks to my wife Lorraine and Mrs Patricia Golden for their efforts in editing this book. Thanks again to Renne Rhea for her art work which became the cover of this book. Thanks to my grandson Dylan S. Tanderup whose image we used to portray Sam Jones the Apache Kid on the cover of this book.

It's 1866 and hundreds of soldiers have been discharged from the Armies of the North and South. Some go home to find nothing for them anymore, while others just never go home. Many flood westward in search of a new life and fresh opportunities. The number of soldiers stationed in the southwest is at its' lowest point in years – the Native Americans known as Apaches are the undisputed rulers of the New Mexico and Arizona Territories.

Chapter One

Sam Jones could feel the sweat pouring down his back as he stood beside his horse looking over the desert. He had been standing in the same spot for more than forty-five minutes. The horse was starting to get restless. Sam moved ever so slightly and pulled on the reins of the bridle just enough to let the big gray horse know that he must continue to stay still.

Since the horse had been with Sam for the last years of the war, he knew the temperament of the man. He had come to know that there was a time for action and a time for waiting. This was a time for waiting quietly. Later he would be fed and well cared for. The gray horse was a good color for a horse to be in the Apache desert. The horses' color blended in well in the barren landscape. There was nothing on the horse or Sam that was flashy or would not blend into the area.

Sam was trying to set his mind straight. He had to start thinking like an Apache. But his mind wandered thinking about his youth for the first time in years, while at the same time watching the hills for any sign of movement. Earlier in the day he had crossed a fresh trail. He had followed it at first, just to be sure there was no threat. Then he realized it was an Apache warrior with a hostage, probably a woman or youngster. Sam knew immediately that he was taking an unnecessary and dangerous risk following the trail. Sort of like playing with a rattlesnake found in your bedroll, it was a good way to get killed. Sam could not help himself, he was drawn to help the captive.

He waited patiently a familiar old feeling made him uneasy. After a while the feeling passed - the Apache had moved on. For some reason this particular Apache seemed to be in a hurry. This was an unusual Apache. Either he had a prize of great value, or he needed to be at some meeting place at some appointed time. The Apache did not think about time as a white man did, it would not be a time but a day. Another thought occurred to Sam; possibly this was a very skilled warrior who was so good that he figured he could ignore the basic rules for fighting in the desert.

An Apache on the run from a raid would ride his horse to death, eat him, and then continue on foot. This Apache had a captive so he apparently was conserving his horse for the captive to ride. Sam followed the trail studying the signs. It was obvious that the Apache was now running alongside the horse. Any Apache warrior could easily run a horse to death.

It finally became apparent to Sam that the Apache was heading for water. All travel in the desert was based around the need for water. The captive needed water soon to survive. It had been years but Sam now remembered where the nearest water was at. It was a risk but there were only a few places in this area.

Sam turned the gray north leaving the trail behind. At first he just walked the horse at a very slow pace, since Sam had no intention of leaving any dust in the air. After he had covered about two miles he started pushing hard. Sam intended to be at the well area long before the Apache warrior arrived with his captive. The Gray seemed to like the desert even though he had never been here before.

Sam was not sure if he was in the New Mexico Territory or the newly formed Arizona Territory, which stretched from

Tucson to Yuma through the heart of the great American Desert. This particular area was hard packed sand covered with sagebrush and tumbleweeds dotting the landscape. Also there were barrel cactus and many of the towering Saguaro cactus. Most think of the desert as being just flat sand, nothing could be further from the truth. There are high mesas, canyons and washes. The entire area was volcanic at one time, with areas so rough and difficult to cross that even the Apache avoid them.

But for all of the roughness and starkness, there was a real beauty. The beauties of wide-open space, clear skies and beautiful mountains. Sam could absorb the beauty in his eyes, listening to the movements and feel the wind, but most of all he absorbed the view through his very being. He could never explain it in words, but the desert was a comfort to him, especially now after three years of war in the East.

Traveling in the southwestern desert of the territory of the United States is a place of constant danger. Rattlesnakes, scorpions, tarantulas, and Gila lizards were just a few of the less perilous creatures. Lack of water and game were the real threats. Of course if one knew where to find game it was then just a matter of staying clear of the most danger predator of the desert - Apaches!

****

Even though it had been over ten years, the old memories came flooding back. Sam had been a young boy when he had first come into this country. He remembered being about five or six following along after the wagon as it went west. For a while the visions of his mother had faded but during the war the memories had come flooding back. Now he could now see the images of her face, as clearly today as he could when he was five. It had taken a lot of effort and concentration, but he had done it. She had been blond just like Sam. She had blue eyes and lovely soft features. Most of all he could remember her voice. She had always read Sam and the other children to sleep. She could sing too. He could still hear her voice and soft songs in his dreams.

Somehow Sam knew that they had moved originally from Kentucky. Sam knew that he had been born there before the family had moved west first to Texas. Times were hard and there was the promise of free land in the new country of Texas. Sam had been very young when the family went to Texas. But then something happened and his father was gone. Sam knew that his father went away for a long time. He now realized that his father had been away fighting in the war against Mexico. When his father returned, all the talk was about going to California.

California was the land of dreams and the discovery of gold. The part of Texas where they had lived must have been in eastern Texas, because Sam's memories were of green hills and grasslands. As they traveled west in a small wagon train, the land gradually became more desolate. West Texas was dry and covered in tumbleweeds. They traveled for weeks and months. Those were good times. Sam could no longer remember who the other families were but they were all nice folks. As they rolled along, some of the men would start to sing some rhyming cadence song then others would join in. There was also music at night Sam remembered his father played a fiddle. He could still remember Pa teaching him how to draw the bow across the strings.

Most of all he remembered his mother. She had a fine singing voice that would carry far into the night. She seemed to know a hundred ballads. They worked hard during the day traveling, but they played and relaxed at night. Maybe there should have been less music and more attention to the details around them.

When they came it was dawn. In typical Apache warfare, they had slipped into concealment positions hours before dawn. When the attack came, there were no war hoops or outcries. It was over in minutes - a good surprise attack. Sam never saw his mother or father killed nor any of his brothers or sisters. He had awakened early and had slipped from his little hammock slung under the wagon. He had gone behind a bush to relieve himself. Years later when he thought about it, he realized they had watched him walk off into the darkness.

The Apache used knives and it was over before anyone woke up. There was one shout that he heard; when he turned, he ran into the Apache who he came to know later as Laglo. He was a big man, who just grabbed Sam and threw him across the horse when he mounted. The ride throughout the day became a nightmare for Sam. Just being carried head down on a fast moving horse is bad enough, but to be taken so abruptly from his family was too much. He did not know it then but Sam had taken the first step on the path to becoming an Apache.

When they arrived in the little village Laglo just threw Sam down. Later, after he understood the language and customs of the Apache, he realized that he should have been honored to be adopted by Laglo, a great warrior. Laglo's woman Deanra had lost her only child several years before. Sam, as a captive, was the replacement for the lost man-child since she apparently was unable to conceive again.

The Apache way of life is that of a raider. Raiders returning with plunder have the sole right to give away all animals of captives taken. Usually to the maternal kinsmen, but also to the rest of the women and elderly not related to the warrior. According to custom, livestock acquired would be evenly distributed among the members of the camp. Sam was just another possession of the raid to be given away, as was Laglo's right.

Apaches lived in *go-tahs* or family camps. Laglo was the most important warrior in this go-tahs. In all, there were seven families in the camp.

His first months of captivity was a time of fear and learning. For the first several months Sam was tied by a leash to Deanra's wrist - everywhere she went so Sam went. He worked alongside her gathering wood, water and herbs. He learned how to cook Apache style and to speak the language. He lost weight, then built muscle. Suddenly one morning before sunrise she cut the leash and told Sam that he now had to take his place with the other boys.

The young boys and girls were watched over by an old warrior, Geto. When not assigned work tasks by the women the boys gathered with Geto. He taught them the things all Apache boys needed to know to become a man. The boys were toughened by strenuous daily exercise. They swam and ran everyday before sunrise. Running was important, so first he had to learn to run as an Apache; the boys ran up the hill and around the camp. Then he had to run to the top of the hill with his mouth full of water; when your mouth is full of water you can only breathe through your nose. Soon the distances were increased and the boys were required to run all day at least once a week. At first Sam was the slowest of the group, but within a year he often was the leader or near the front. This pleased both Laglo and Deanra.

There were two other boys in another family who became Sam's companions; Prumi and Tatsahdago. Prumi was about a year younger than Sam, whereas Tatsahdago was about a year older. At first Sam was always the odd man out at any game. No one wanted him on their team or even to run against him in an individual contest.

One morning he was out gathering wood when he could hear a cry for help. It was Tatsahdago, he had fallen in a rattlesnake pit. There were hundreds. Tatsahdago was cornered up on a rock with no way out. Sam built a fire as he had been taught, then carefully he lit small lengths of wood on fire. Sam entered the pit laying the burning sticks in a line making a path through the enraged snakes. Tatsahdago would have been embarrassed to have the story told that he had been in such a predicament. But Sam never said a word or ever made reference to the incident.

After that, Tatsahdago always insisted that Sam be on his team, soon the two brothers and Sam became inseparable. Over the years they became close friends, they hunted and fished together. The three talked about adventures, girls about the goals of becoming Apache warriors, and everything else young boys talk about.

Geto also taught the boys the skills all warriors should have, especially the bow and the knife. Sam learned to hunt with the bow, spear, or a knife. He learned to set traps, snares and to harvest the eatable plants of the desert.

Sam learned the games played by the other boys – the hoop game as well as hide and seek. But Apache boy games are more than just games, they teach the boys the many skills needed to become a warrior and a raider. Hide and seek taught the boys to conceal themselves in plain sight, how to hold a position for hours and to take advantage of every bit of cover available. Later when the boys and girls became proficient at hide and seek, they learned the art of stealing horses or mules. Apaches pride themselves on being the best at stealing a horse or any livestock for that matter. Sam became one of the best. Once he even took a horse while the man held the reins in his sleeping hand – that impressed the brothers.

****

Sam arrived first. It was not much of a water hole, in fact later in the year it would be dry. It was just a small outcrop of rocks where water would well up from a source far below the surface. Sam could not remember what the place was called, he just remembered where it was. This was water known only to the Apache, so the warrior coming in would not be expecting anyone to be waiting. Sam remembered enough of the Apache way to know that any Apache would be alert and ready for anything approaching such a place.

Sam had left his big gray horse more than a mile away since the horse would be more than likely to give away their presence. Sam looked over all of the obvious places to watch the water. Then he picked one of the less obvious places to watch from. Even though he was thirsty Sam made no attempt to approach the water. There was no way he could get water without leaving signs for the other man to see.

The hours passed and the sun went down. The darkness enveloped Sam, then the moon came up. Suddenly, there he was, just standing by the water hole. The big Apache allowed the horse to drink first while he watched the area for any sign of danger. Then he pulled the woman down in one swift motion and allowed her to drink. Finally, he knelt and dipped his hand for a drink. The woman spoke saying something that Sam could not hear, but this caused the Apache to turn his attention toward her momentarily. It was long enough; Sam moved fast and grabbed the big Apache from behind.

It was not quite so simple. The warrior must have sensed something because he moved just before Sam tried to drive in a fatal blow using his knife. The warrior tried to throw Sam with a rolling hip throw, but Sam stomped his instep and foiled that. Sam lost his death grip on the warrior's throat. It had been years since he had fought another Apache, but instinct took over as he felt the man move. The Apache had his knife in hand when he came around facing Sam.

The two blades clanged together in the quiet of the desert. This was the sound that alerted the woman to the battle. The Apache lunged at Sam - Sam surprised him by catching his wrist and rolling backwards, using his legs and feet to flip the big Apache through the air. This was an Apache fighter the warrior realized - *it would be a great victory to defeat such an opponent.* The Apache twisted in midair and landed on his feet in a crouch. There was no fear just the look of determination.

Sam could see the streak of red on the Apache's side; he had managed to draw blood. Blades clanged again as Sam thrust this time. They rolled in the sand, then came up locked together. Each trying to get a better foothold in the soft sand so the other could be pushed down. Both were strong and able having already blocked the surprise attacks.

A rock under Sam's left foot threw him off balance - the Apache came in for the kill. *Sam desperately needed some type of advantage at this point, so he spoke to the Apache in his own language.*

"You fight like a woman. An Owl must ride on your back."

The warrior hesitated, not only from the surprise of the Anglo being able to speak the language, but also from the words of dark magic. Sam surged up and thrust his knife in just under the breastbone. The Apache was dead, but he remained standing.

The Apache asked a final question.

"Who is this great warrior who speaks of Owls?"

"I am the son of Laglo and Deanra." He spoke using precise words of the Apache people.

The Apache warrior collapsed and died with a look of disbelief on his face.

The girl screamed.

"Be quiet," Sam said curtly, in English.

She gasped, "I thought you were another one of them."

"Well I'm not. Just be quiet and still. I want to be sure that he was alone."

Sam faded into the night and circled the area slowly. He could not sense any other presence. When he came back to the edge of the water she was just sitting there crying.

"Are you hurt," Sam asked?

"No, I don't think so," she replied trying to sniff up the tears.

"Then what is the matter?"

"I - I don't know. It's been such a long day. You left me with a dead Indian. I thought you might not come back."

Sam understood; he placed his hand on her shoulder to give some comfort and reassurance. "It's all right. I understand. Don't worry, I'll not leave you out here."

Now she got angry. Not only was she embarrassed for crying but she had been scared all day. Now came the realization that Sam had killed the other man so brutally, and now apparently his tone told her that he thought no more about killing the Apache than if he had stepped on a pesky insect. "How can you understand?"

"I too, was captured by the Apache. My family was killed."

"I'm sorry, I guess you do know what it's like."

"No time for chit-chat now." Sam was thinking about their situation. He needed his horse and he needed to eat, she probably did too. "We can't stay here. Before we leave we need to take care of things."

"Okay," the girl was starting to settle down now. "What do you want me to do?"

"Take his pouch and blanket from the horse. We are going to need that horse."

She started to speak but Sam had already walked away. Sam grabbed the dead warrior by the feet and dragged him away from the water. There was a crack in the surface of the ground that would do, it was just wide enough for a man's body. Sam rolled the body down into the opening. He tossed in the

Apache's knife and bow. She had the blanket and saddle off of the horse. Sam took both and threw them into the hole covering the man.

"I have to go and get my horse. Can you scoop in enough sand to cover him while I'm gone?"

"What do I use?"

Sam handed her a piece of wood that he had found. It was not much but it was wide and flat on one end. It could be used as a makeshift shovel.

"I'll do my best. Please hurry." She pleaded.

"I will." He promised.

The Apache and their close kinsmen, the Navajos, belong to the widespread Athapascan linguistic family of Native Americans - believed to part of the last migratory wave from Asia just before the Eskimos. No one is really certain when the ancestral groups of Apaches reached the GREAT southwest desert; however it is believed that the region's climate changed significantly between 800 and 1200, probably sometime after that the Apache moved into the area displacing other inhabitants. Nevertheless the Apache were thoroughly at home and acclimated to the region when the Spanish arrived in the late 1500's.

Chapter Two

As the first light of day came through she could gradually see the bulk of the man ahead of her. He was not that tall but his shoulders seemed to be wider than any she had ever seen. When he stopped, her horse came up even with him and she could see him clearly for the first time. His hair was blond, almost white. There was no indication that he had seen a barber recently; his hair was bushy and over his ears. The youthful appearance in his face showed that he shaved rarely. His penetrating eyes were pale blue, which seemed to change color when he looked hard at her. She felt at times he seemed to be able to look right through her. Scars on the side of his face and another on the side of his neck were indicators of past battles. His nose had been broken at one time, but it was not unpleasantly out of place with the rest of his chiseled looking features.

He was wearing a buckskin coat with the sleeves cut off up high on the shoulder. His shirt had probably been red at one time but now appeared as a rust color. The trousers she recognized by the stripe; they were U.S. Army Calvary issues. There was a tear where the Apache had cut his jacket, but otherwise his clothes had been mended and taken care of. His hat was wide brimmed and old but still well creased. Everything he wore was drab and seemed to blend in with the stark landscape.

The man was heavily armed. He carried two pistols that she could see. One in a holster on his waist rigged for what was referred to as cross draw, another larger pistol was in a saddle holster on the horse within easy reach. He carried a short rifle in the cross of his arm, she seemed to recall her father calling it a Spencer. Another rifle stuck out from the boot at the rear of his horse. She recognized it because she had only seen one other - it was a Henry-repeating rifle. He carried two wicked looking knives, one sticking out from his right boot top and another, larger, a Bowie slung across his back. She was curious as to which of the knives he had used to dispatch the Apache last night. The arsenal was ominous.

They had been riding for hours throughout the night since leaving the waterhole. In all that time he had never spoken, even when he returned with his horse. He had just gone to work helping her to finish scooping sand over the grave of the Apache warrior. Then he mounted and rode his horse back and forth over the grave from several directions. Then he cantered his horse around the water hole while leading her horse. He allowed both horses to drink while filling all of the water bags and canteens, they were off.

After the long hours of silence she was somewhat startled when he spoke to her. "You doing all right," he asked?

"I'm just fine," she replied, more as a direct answer trying to be polite rather than telling the truth. In fact, she was so tired she was ready to fall off the horse. Her more recent experiences had affected her - she knew that she did not dare to show weakness now. Somehow she needed to find some inner strength to go on.

She watched him as he looked carefully sweeping the horizon then the ground in-between. More than a full minute elapsed before he answered.

"That's good. It's best to go on until it starts to get hot. Then we will rest during the heat of the day." He was looking at her. "You have a name girl?"

She realized he was looking her over in the light of the morning also; just as she had been doing with him. She flushed with a little embarrassment - she must look a sight. Her hair was not done - it must be simply wild and her clothing was torn and filthy from dirt and sweat. Of course there is nothing lady like in the way she was riding astride on the horse with her dress pulled up to the knees. Well, she still had some dignity. She pulled herself upright in the saddle.

"I am Elizabeth Ann Ridgway. My father is General Ridgway commanding the southern Army forces in California. I probably should feel lucky that you realized my father is an important man so I was worthy of being rescued."

"Well, Elizabeth Ridgway." He hesitated and spat out a pebble from his mouth. "Since I did not know your name - I certainly could not know you were the daughter of General Ridgway; whoever he might be. But, for your information, it would not have mattered if you were the daughter of a General or dirt farmer; I still would have not wanted Prumi back there to have you."

"You knew the Indian who carried me

off?"   She   was   incredulous.   "You
killed a man you knew so cruelly!"

"We   played   together   as   children.
However, until I spoke to him he did
not   remember   me.   That   was   the
advantage I got in the fight, sometimes
it makes the difference. Just remember
no matter how cruelly he died, your
death would have been even crueler by
his hands. Out here in the West it is
a tough brutal world.   The desert is
even more so. If you wanted nice you
should have stayed back East."

She had no idea how to respond to
this strange man, so she changed the
subject. "How may I address you?"

"Sorry, I'm, Sam. Sam Jones."

"Beth," She replied.

"Beth?"

"My father and friends call me Beth,
not   Elizabeth.   Since   we   seem   to
traveling in the same direction and you
saved me from who knows what, it seems
only proper that I allow you to address
me by my first name."

"Okay Beth, it is."   He chuckled at
her arrogance.

She was still curious, "Why did you
bury the Apache you killed and leave
the grave unmarked."

"You sure ask a lot of questions. I
guess that is just natural. The burial
you saw is the Apache way. Once an
Apache dies he or she is never spoken

of again, the name is gone forever. An Apache who dies is buried immediately after death with every possession he has. There is no funeral - once the people who bury the one that has died return, they burn their clothes and bathe in 'ghost smoke' made from sage. Anything that cannot be buried with him is destroyed. The family moves and the go-tah where they have been living is burned. Any children of the deceased usually have their names changed. Death is never a topic of conversation, and all graves are unmarked and the location is kept as secret, known only to the ones who actually performed the burial."

"So why bury the Indian at all?"

"First to leave a body at a water hole just creates the possibility of tainting the entire water supply of others and the animals in the area. Also, by burying him when his own people find him missing, they will realize that we honored his abilities as a warrior and properly concealed his body. But, most of all, an exposed body attracts varmints and vultures. That will put them on our trail that much sooner."

"On our trail? How will they find us?" This renewed the fright.

"After a raid, they all break away and go in different directions. But they were due to meet somewhere at a specific time. When he fails to show they will backtrack, locate his trail and follow us. Oh, they will not dig him up but they will go to the water hole and they will find his trail in but none leaving. As for finding us, that is the easy part - there are only so many places to get water. When we get water they will find us."

"I thought it was all over."

"No it's just the beginning."

As they moved out, her thoughts drifted to better times.

****

She had lived most of her life following her father from one Army post to another. Beth's father was a professional soldier, a graduate of West Point and greatly respected. Her earliest memories were of playing with the other children in the post compound of a fort. Laramie, Pittsburgh and many others, they all seemed to be the same. They were there for a while then gone to find new playmates at another fort. She had lost count of the number of times the cycle had repeated.

Beth's mother was a very pretty woman who was every bit the lady. Very charming and religious; Beth loved her dearly. As she got older, Beth had somewhat resented her mother's attitude, because she had always just taken each move in stride. In time, she also learned that she was the daughter of an officer in the dragoons; much to her dismay her mother monitored all of her friends, to ensure that all were in the proper social standing.

Beth was born after her father returned from the Mexican-American War so she had no concepts of war until the Civil War started. When the war started they had been in Fort Laramie. Her father decided it would be best if everyone returned to his home in Philadelphia. Once there, Beth was enrolled in the all girls' school at Worthington. 'A proper school for young ladies of her social status,' her mother called it.

Her father went off to war and came back a month later wounded in the arm. His left arm had to be amputated. She noticed right away the change in her mother. There were fewer conversations, less parties, and her mother spent more time in church. While her father was recuperating, she came to know him for the first time. He was primarily an engineer who wanted to build bridges and grand roads. As such he started telling her about his visions of bridges that could span many miles of rivers and across great gorges. Nothing in her school spoke of such things.

When her father went back to the army her mother took to her bed. The reports of battles and killing were in all the papers; it seemed that each battle brought on even more horrifying news. Then her mother came down with pneumonia. It was on a warm summer night, the last of June, 1863, when her mother died. She sent a message, but there was no answer from her father. During the first four days of July, the fate of the nation was decided at a battle called Gettysburg. Her father was there and involved in the thick of battle. Therefore, it was left to Beth to make all of the arrangements for her mother. Then the reports came flowing in about Gettysburg, and for two days she feared the worst, that both of her parents had perished. The next day her father came home to stand with her at the funeral - he was now a Brigadier General.

Things changed after that, her father was reassigned to Washington D.C. They moved from Philadelphia and he placed her in the Chatom School for girls. Here she was exposed for the first time to actual subjects that interested her. Even though her father was vastly involved in the day-to-day operations of supporting the war, he still came home each evening and made time to spend with her. Slowly the horrors of war and the stark realities of her mother's passing started to fade. In a way, this became a very happy time in her life.

One evening she came home from school to find her father already there. It was far too early for dinner. He was quite upset, but all decisions had been made. He had been reassigned to California. It was only a matter of time before the war was over. He had decided to go on ahead without her. He explained that the future was in the west and he would send for her when the term at school ended or if the war ended.

The War ended in April and two months later, in June, school was out. The Army still controlled all transportation, and she was informed it was not safe to travel. Everything was booked solid anyway, so after waiting for more than three months she finally booked passage to Independence by stage. More weeks more of waiting passed, then finally passage was been booked to San Diego. Even so she had been force to spend a month in Santa Fe because of the danger from Apache Indians.

While in Santa Fe Beth had heard the horrible tales about the Apache, but she had dismissed them. Somehow, Beth had convinced herself that the stories were exaggerated - after all, she had been around Indians her whole life and she had no fear of them. When the Apaches had attacked the stage, it was

over in less than a minute. They had
not come in riding and whooping in a
cloud of dust. It was sudden; first
they were not there then they were all
around. The stage had slowed to climb
the crest of a long hill, the driver
walked the team. Finally, the driver
stopped and ordered all passengers out
of the coach, and directed them to walk
alongside. One man stayed on top of
the coach with a rifle on guard as the
driver took the reins and walked also.
She had glanced down, heard a muffled
scream and then Prumi was standing in
front of her.

She started to scream also but he
muffled her voice with his hand. She
saw the carnage in the moments of her
abduction. The driver had been killed
along with the guard in the first
moments of the battle - She did not see
the others being killed but she saw the
other men dead in pools of blood when
they rode away. It took only a few
minutes for the Apache to take the
horses, loot the luggage, and push the
stage over the cliff. Then Prumi had
thrown her face down over the neck of
his horse and then rode for hours. He
was such a strong forceful man that he
had left her bruised on every spot
where he had touched her body.

Now she was with this man. A man
that she knew nothing about other than
the dramatic killing of her abductor -

this man that seemed almost as violent as the one who had abducted and abused her.

****

It was starting to get warm, though not too warm, as it was still early in the year. By June or July the heat during the day would peak at over a hundred degrees every day. There had been rain and the winter desert was green. Sam could see all the signs of an early spring; there had not been that much rain. There were flowers on the cacti, bees moved all around and birds were nesting.

He looked back she was almost asleep in the saddle. It was time to stop. For the first time he studied her. He decided that she was a very pretty girl. Even with the dirt smudges on her face it was a pleasant face to look at. Her eyes were a dark blue, almost violet, especially when her temper was up. She had long reddish blond hair that he had heard described as strawberry blond. Her nose was a little big but it went well with her high cheekbones. Her skin was pale and starting to burn in the brutal sun. He would have to get her a hat. She was not too short, but she was nowhere as tall as he was - he figured she was somewhere around 5 foot 5 inches. She had all the female curves in the right places and had a well-developed chest for a girl her size. He had not been around many women, but he liked what he saw.

He found a good place in a jumble of rocks. The rocks would provide good shade and protection from the heat. Of course there would be no water here, but he had carefully filled all water bags before leaving. A rabbit scurried out ahead of the horses. There was no temptation on his part to shoot it, even though they would need meat. Any noise would be heard for miles in the sill desert air.

He pulled up halting the horses, she snapped awake. "Where are we?"

"A good place to rest."

She watched admiring his smooth grace and agility as he came off his horse. He stepped back and reached up for her. She took his hand without hesitation and allowed him to assist her. "I'm hungry. Do we have anything to eat?"

"The supplies are limited but the desert provides an abundance of items."

"There is nothing out here but snakes and cactus."

"That is not really true, but both in general are edible," he replied softly.

"I could never eat such disgusting things." She snapped back.

"Most people will eat anything if they are hungry enough!"

"Really Mr. Jones."

He did not answer but went right to work; first he scouted the entire area on foot. He found a safe spot for her to do her business and motioned for her. He left her and went about caring for the horses. Since the horses were the so critical to their survival, he paid special attention to them. After stripping them he rubbed them down with a plant removing any stickers. Each was watered and fed. He had been stopping and picking grass and other greens while they had been traveling. This was the food for the horses.

When she returned he had the camp set up. He rolled out his bedroll in the shade and motioned for her to use his bedroll.

"Please Mr. Jones I can't."

"Don't worry, I have an extra blanket." He separated it from the bedroll and placed it nearby in another shady spot.

He removed his jacket and laid down on the blanket using the jacket for a pillow. He covered his eyes with his hat. She sat on the bedroll and worked on her hair. It was full of sand. She worked on the worst of the knots and snarls. It was hopeless without a brush or comb.

"So, Mr. Jones what do you do when you are not saving kidnapped women?"

Now, for some reason she was not sleepy.

He picked up his hat and looked out at her. "You had better rest. We will be traveling all night tonight."

"You did not answer my question."

"Well I guess you could say that I am unemployed."

"You just wander around the desert?"

"I am traveling to California."

"I noticed that you are wearing Union Calvary pants."

"Yes, I was a soldier in the War. When I was discharged I decided to go to California."

"You were an officer in the Union Army Calvary?"

"No, a Sergeant Major. A scout on General Grant's staff for the past two years."

She had spent years around Army posts, all the Sergeant Majors she had known had been middle aged. "You appear too young to be a Sergeant Major," she noted.

"Well, the war makes them promote young."

She remembered her father talking about some of the officers who had been promoted rapidly and they too were very young; advanced rapidly even to the rank of Brigadier General. He had been quite vocal about Custer and the others; the men he called boy generals. These young Generals, who had been very valiant in battle had been swiftly promoted beyond their years; it made sense that it had also occurred within the enlisted ranks. Maybe there was something special about this man Sam Jones.

"You did not ask me about how I was captured?"

"Figured you would tell me when you were ready. Don't need to know where the rock fell from to catch it. It's an easy assumption everyone with you was killed or Prumi would not have gotten you."

"So what are you going to do in California?"

"This is the last question. Then we sleep. I plan to start a ranch."

With that, he covered his eyes and lay still and his breathing changed and she knew he was asleep. She laid down thinking that she was not really sleepy and it was going to be hard to sleep in the daylight. Moments later, sleep took her.

Andrew Johnson from Tennessee, a democrat is President of the United States. He became President when Abraham Lincoln was assassinated. As President Johnson tries to implement the reconstruction plan laid out by Lincoln he comes into conflict with the Republican dominated congress. Those Army units not involved in the occupation of the South have been shipped to the west to contain the Indian problems which have been mostly ignored during the years of war.

Chapter Three

Jock looked over the area carefully before approaching. The stage lay on its side, the horses were gone, and what had been the luggage was opened and routed through and was strewn about. This was an old story in this territory - an attack by Apache and everyone killed.

Eventually, he moved from his concealment and walked carefully through the ravaged area. All of the men had been killed brutally as was the Apache way. *Well at least they went fast*, he thought. *There was not a good way to go but if you had to go it's better to go fast, and not let the Apache take their time. When the Apache took their time with captives the results of torture are gruesome. Probably these folks only had an instant to realize what had happened.*

He could see from the signs clearly what had happened as if he had actually watched the attack. It was a perfect area for attack - just like he would have picked. Out in the open with little concealment, the men were probably looking outward towards the horizon line more than a hundred yards away. He found a spot where a warrior had laid in a shallow depression. *Hiding in plain sight,* Jock concluded without even thinking about it. The Apache had probably followed the stage for hours or maybe even a day. Then ran ahead and waited for hours. At the right time they came out of the ground literally and killed everyone - probably within a half a minute.

The he saw it and he had a sinking feeling in the pit of his stomach - A woman's shoe. He had not seen the body of a woman. His first thought was, *'by now she would be wishin she was dead'*.

There was a shovel in the boot of the wagon, Jock did not say a word. He just grabbed the shovel and started digging. It took hours to dig seven graves – the ground was not that soft after you got down a foot or so. He stripped off his leather jacket and shirt and dug bare chested. He looked down at the wisps of hair on his chest. They were white and grey, just like the little remaining hair on his head. He kept his hat on, this was no time to get a sunburn on his head. Jock was a little man, about five six with a small frame, weighing only about one fifty on a good day. But, he was strong. He had been fighting and working hard his entire life. He had no idea how old he was, but he had marched with Andrew Jackson from Tennessee when he was probably around fourteen, although he had told them he was sixteen. He had fought the Creeks then eventually served at the Battle of New Orleans.

But then he had been drawn to the west and had lived as a trapper all during the twenties and thirties. It had been a good life - but like everything it changed. He had driven stage, worked as a bullwhacker with a freighting outfit, hunted for gold during the California rush of '49, and had even been a bouncer at one of the more upper class whore houses in San Francisco. He had fought in at least two-dozen Indian battles and had lived among the Indians. Jock liked the Indians and their way of life, and had even married a native beauty - the first of his three wives. Now he was a scout for the Army, mostly because he did not have to punch cattle nor be a farmer; two vocations he totally disliked. Being a scout was not a job without risks, but by his figuring he had to be just shy of sixty, and he surly could not get an easier job at his age.

He also remembered the three women that he had married; he had also dug their graves along with the grave of his baby son. Now he would have no son to dig his grave, but the Army would dig him a grave no matter what. He had decided a long time ago that he wanted to be buried somewhere in the high lonesome and there would be no need for a marker, because he alone knew what he had done and not done. He struggled but finally drug the men into the holes.

Seven men buried in a row wrapped in their blankets. He stacked rocks on top of the graves to keep the varmints from digging. At last the job was done. He was just finishing when he could hear the approaching wagons of the Army convoy.

****

As the wagons came in sight Jock could see Sergeant Von Chek in the lead. Jock did not care much for the man who thought much of his own abilities, yet knew so little about Indians and even less about Apache. Von Chek was a brute of a man with fists of iron. Jock had seen him pummel men into submission. Von Chek also disliked Jock - referring to Jock as undisciplined and unwashed. The first was probably true but the second was not. Von Chek held up his hand to halt the column and stopped about ten feet from Jock.

"I see the little man has done some work for a change. Hard to believe you would get your hands dirty." Von Chek slurred his words in a thick German accent. Jock just looked at the man. "You did not put any markers on the graves."

Jock took off his hat and wiped his baldhead with his bandanna. "Well, these fellers didn't bother to give me their names. An as for gittin my hands dirty; I'd even dirty my hands to dig a grave for you, Sergeant."

The silly grin came off Sergeant Von Chek's face as he flushed, realizing that Jock had somehow insulted him. He started to dismount, thinking as to get down and make an issue with Jock. Before he could make up his mind two riders came up from the rear. Second Lieutenant Evans and Sergeant Major MacPherson. Lieutenant Evans was a recent graduate of West Point and this was actually his first assignment. He was young thin, in good shape and cut a dashing figure in his tailor made uniform. MacPherson on the other hand was even bigger than Von Chek, a burly man, an obvious descendant from hearty Scotch stock.

Lieutenant Evans looked around and then spoke to Jock, "Apache?"

Jock had picked up the shovel during his exchange with Von Chek, figuring to use it on the man if necessary. So now he just leaned against it. "Yep. Maybe ten or a dozen. Left the strong box and mail, probably ought to carry it to someone."

Lieutenant Evans nodded and looked at Von Chek, "Have the men recover anything of value so we can report this."

"Yes Sir", the Sergeant replied. He might not like Jock but he would not make an issue in front of the Lieutenant or MacPherson.

Jock finished briefing the Lieutenant and Big MacPherson after Von Chek had left, about finding the stage and passengers along with their state and his conclusions on how the battle had occurred. When Jock finished, MacPherson had a feeling so he asked, "Is there anything else?"

Jock nodded, "There were eight on the stage. I believe the Patch carried off a girl or woman."

"God help her," Corporal Juan Vargas tersely; while at the same time he crossed himself as was the Catholic way.

All the men seemed to agree with silent grim looks.

"It's getting late," MacPherson said, looking at the sun starting to bring long shadows. "Probably only about another hour or so of light."

Jock pointed to a mound of rocks further up, "There's water and good area for protection. Only about a half hour if we shake a leg." The Lieutenant nodded and walked off, the others had drifted off too, getting things ready to move out again. Jock pulled on his shirt and jacket, then watched as two troopers picked up the strongbox and mailbag.

MacPherson motioned to Jock. When they were alone he asked, "Would these Apache attack a large, well-armed military column like ours."

"Patches ain't skerd of nothing and we ain't that big to impress them. They's notional – they could take a notion if they thought we had something they needed."

"Like guns."

"Oh, yea; guns would do it."

****

She woke at his touch on her arm.

"Time to go," he said in a low tone.

She watched as he efficiently broke the camp and stored everything. "Can I help?" she offered.

"Sorry, I guess I'm just so a custom to doing everything myself that I tend to ignore anyone else. It's all done now."

She stood "I'm hungry. Can we cook something?"

"No fire." He reached into a

bag and pulled out some dry jerky.

"Here." He handed her the clump of meat. "We will move out and you can eat on the way."

He then did the most curious thing. He carefully brushed out all evidence of where they had been. Then he walked the horses backwards, carefully along the same path that they had approached the rock pile from. After a hundred yards, where they had crossed a dry creek bed, he walked forward, veering off along the soft sand leading the horses in a single file. He went back and carefully poured sand in the imprints left.

"Will that fool them?" She inquired.

Sam was getting adjusted to her frequent questions. He realized that she really knew practically nothing about anything out here. "I doubt it, but it might slow them down some, particularly if a wind storm comes along before they do."

"Where are we going?"

"I think that Fort Bowie is out there somewhere on the other side of the pass. If we miss that, Fort Lowell is by Tucson." He stopped and reached into his saddle bag and pulled out a folded package wrapped in oil skin. He withdrew a map and placed it against the rump of her horse. He pointed before speaking, "I believe we are somewhere in here. If we miss the forts we will go into Tucson."

"That looks like an Army map." Her tone accused.

"It is - I traded for it." He carefully folded the map and replaced it. "Eat your dinner." He vaulted onto the horse and led her horse.

She had never tried jerked meat before it was terrible. At first, she attempted to chew. It was just too hard so she just held it in her mouth and sucked on it. It helped, soon the meat soften up and her stomach started feeling better.

So into the night they went. It became another nightmare for Beth. The altitude in the mountains is up over four thousand feet. They crossed over along the continental divide during the night and the temperatures dropped into the forties. It was cold - damn cold. Sam took out the blanket and placed it over her shoulders. It helped, but her legs were still cold."

As daylight approached, she could see something of the new country they were crossing. They had gone from the flat sagebrush and tumbleweed-covered plain to the rocky jumbled hills. These hills were alive with game and other creatures. Twice she saw deer and once a sheep ram standing proudly on a rocky butte. There was still cactus, which had also changed; a reminder that they were still in the desert.

He walked his horse and stopped often. She had been dosing on and off throughout the night but now, they just stood in the sunrise, not moving. To her this was a very grossly inefficient method of travel.

She asked quietly, "What are we waiting for?"

"I am trying to get the feel of

things. By listening, smelling and looking carefully we might stay alive."

Beth remarked, "I don't hear anything except the rustling of the sage as the wind blows. As for smell, there is only this horse."

"You have not been taught to use all senses as any child Apache has. I can hear a snake crawling over there." He pointed at a clump of bushes to the northwest. "As for smell - I can smell you, your horse, mine, and the skunk that came by several hours ago."

They moved out at a walking pace and covered maybe another mile until he halted again. He pulled out a stick from his saddle and strung the bow. From a small pouch, he produced an arrow, which he notched in place. Now he was just sitting in his saddle, he looked relaxed, almost asleep. She realized this was a façade - he was on alert and ready. Fear crept into her! Did he sense an enemy? Then with one smooth motion he pulled back the bow and let go. She could not see what he had shot, but something was making noise around a bush. He walked the horses forward, leaned over from the saddle and lifted the still form of a rabbit in one smooth motion.

"Meat today." Sam stated softly as he urged the horses forward to a large clump of rocks and jumped down. "We will risk a small fire, since there has been no indication of pursuit. Come down its time to take a break."

She swung down and watched as he quickly skinned the rabbit and gutted it. He buried the entrails and then built a small fire over the spot. Sam rubbed dry sage and salt over the meat. Soon the smell of roasting meat was noticeable. While the meat cooked, he cared for the horses and then worked on the rabbit skin.

"Are we going to rest here?" Beth questioned.

"Only for an hour or so. There is water a couple hours ahead. We will not be able to cook at the water, so we will eat and move on. I would not normally stop, but the horses need water."

The rabbit was delicious. She

was unsure if it was because she had not eaten for almost a day or if the rabbit was well prepared.

They moved out an hour later with full bellies. Sam was trying to remember this area. It had been so long ago. The last time he was in this area he had been with Prumi and Tatsahdago.

The year 1865 had been bad in the southwest; disastrous weather, plant disease, and insects destroyed many crops. The Mescaleros had been placed on reservations with their long standing enemies, the Navajos. In November, the Mescaleros with any strength, departed the reservation for the mountain strongholds. They would rather die in the mountains with dignity than be starved by the Anglos.

Chapter Four

The sign was written in black letters probably with charcoal on the little cabin door. The scrawl read:

No silver - No gold

100 miles to next water

20 miles to wood

6 inches to hell

Gone to Calif.

Enter at your own risk!

Someone had built a crude cabin in the middle of the little cup of a basin next to the water hole. The last time Sam had been here this cabin had not been here. There was no place to cut any wood so a lot of effort had been expended hauling the logs here from the nearby mountains. A crude chimney had been built from lava rocks.

The girl jumped down and started for the door.

"Hold up," Sam called out.

"What's the matter now? Do you always have to be so bossy?"

"It's best to go slow. Did you notice the rattlesnake by the door?"

Beth jumped back as if she had sat on a hot rock. "Why didn't you tell me?"

"Never gave me a chance. Just be careful."

Sam dropped off his horse in his easy manner landing on both feet. He moved around the cabin looking it over carefully. There were no windows but the chinking had been left off in several key areas that would allow anyone in the cabin to look through and shoot from if needed. Sam waited patiently while the snake moved on. There was no other sign of motion. Sam was careful, something about this situation made him wary.

Finally, he entered the cabin.

Apparently empty, it was only one room over a dirt floor. The entire room was about twenty by twenty. The fireplace took up one wall. A bed with no mattress, made of hand carved posts and a leather bottom lashed to the posts, sat next to the far wall. Crudely built cupboards were on the other wall across from the fireplace. A lone chair sat by a table. Both had been constructed well by a good workman, but both were in poor shape from being abandoned. There was no evidence of danger.

Sam motioned for Beth as he stepped out. "Go ahead check it out. I need to scout around." Sam moved out at a trot. He covered the entire basin. The water actually flowed from an upper basin within the jumble of rocks down to the pool by the cabin. Finally, he decided that they were alone. As he came back down, he noticed that Beth's horse was drinking from the pool. His grey was standing clear of the water. He ran fast towards the horse but it was too late. Now he knew what the problem was the water was tainted. The big grey was too smart to drink. The other horse was now doomed - it was just a matter of time.

Sam sniffed the water. He was angry with himself he should have caught it. He waved the stupid horse back and waded into the pool. It was only knee deep - it took less than a minute to find the box. It was heavy; it took everything he had to drag the box from the pond. The girl came from the cabin.

"What did you find?"

"Poison."

"What kind of Poison?"

"Don't know."

Sam dragged the box clear of the water. It was an old steamer trunk. He unlatched the lid and opened it. Both stared intently into the box. A strong acid odor rolled out."

Beth coughed from the stench. "What is it?"

"Chemicals used in assay for mining, I believe," Sam said.

"Why would anyone put it in the pond?" Her tone displayed incredulity.

"Sheer meanness!" Sam groused.

The stupid horse reared and blew. Sam caught up the horse and led him away into the desert.

"Where are you going with my horse?" She followed, almost running to keep up.

"He is going to die. I will not allow him to suffer."

She stopped realizing what was about to happen. She did not want to watch him kill the sick horse.

There was a time, he remembered, *that he was more alert and would have never allowed the horse to drink. Had he allowed himself to be distracted by the girl? Well he had better get over any distractions if they were going to survive the desert and the Apache.*

****

After living with the Apache for more than five years, Sam was known by the name Kikna. He spoke only Apache and thought only in the language of the Apache people. As the years passed memories of his past life faded into the dreams of the night. The three young warriors were not yet considered men. It took four raids to become an Apache warrior. The boys were eleven and soon would be allowed to go on raids.

The three Apache lads had stolen some fine horses. Then, on a lark, had ridden north to see the strange Americans who were so different from the hated Mexican-Spaniards. All the boys had been warned to avoid the Mexicans since they captured Indians and used them as slaves. This treatment would be considered worse than death. The other big danger is scalp hunters. The Mexican government pays twenty-five pesos for every scalp. Bands of scalp hunters roam the southwest and northern Mexico in search of scalps.

On the second day, the boys came upon a remote ranch. First, they watched the men working the cattle. It would have been good to steal cattle and drive them back, but there were just too many men. Apache warriors detest heroics, they seek to gain an overwhelming advantage or surprise. If the boys could not get into a favorable position to slip in to get the cattle, then it would be a foolish risk.

They moved on and found the main ranch house. Here they found a different situation. With all the men gone, it was just a lone woman and her children. They watched all day as she went about her chores; washing clothes, cleaning, chopping wood, and even playing with the children.

Now the boys focused their attention on the horses in the far corral. There must have been more than twenty. To return with this prize would be a real trophy. Prumi teased Sam by pointing out that the American squaw had light yellow hair just like him. Sam had always been sensitive to his differences. Now he fought down the challenge that his friend presented.

It was only an hour until sunset. Tatsahdago wanted to go in and kill the squaw along with the children; then take the horses. Sam knew of no vengeance oath against these people, after all, they were not the hated Mexicans engaged in scalping and slavery. So Sam proposed that it

would be a very good joke, to
just slip in take all the horses
during the night, with the empty
corral to be discovered in the
morning. Prumi smiled, he agreed
that it would indeed be a very
good joke. This would be a deed
that could be told with pride -
anyone could kill a woman or
children.

This was the Apache way. The
Apache had been raiders since the
Spanish had first come into this
country. The Apache had been
great hunters, but after the
Spanish arrived, they had for
generations become raiders.
Small groups, no more than five
to twelve, went out usually on
foot and located horses or
cattle. They would follow for
days, waiting for the proper
opportunity, then sneak in and
drive off the herd. Raiding was
not war, just a way to feed the
family. War was for revenge.

It was an evening of stealth,
but the first light of morning
found the three Apache lads
driving a herd of twenty-two,
head miles from the ranch. *Their
first stop was at the waterhole
where the little cabin now stood.*

****

Beth woke bathed in sweat; she was alone. His empty bed role lay next to hers. She placed her hand on his blanket - it was still warm. He had not been gone long. She looked around trying to locate him.

The jumbled rocks that surrounded the cabin created long shadows in the twilight. She peered in each of the shadows trying to find the man. But to no avail-the man was like a shadow himself. As she circled around on her search she suddenly heard a noise. It was just a rustling noise, but she jumped back from it anyway, without crying out; she was learning. Now she saw the snake, just a little one. She fell back in her haste to get away, landing on her rump. She took a few deep breaths and focused - on the sandy ground just in front of her was another creature even more horrid than a snake.

Beth had never before seen a tarantula. The sight of a spider bigger than her hand brought instant terror - now she screamed. The spider jumped landing right in her lap. Before she could scream again Sam was there. He scooped up the big spider holding it from above. Sam walked over to the edge of the clearing and tossed the spider.

Tears streamed down her cheeks. "Did you kill that thing?"

"You must have scared it pretty bad or it would not have jumped at you."

"I scared the spider? – I think I just lost what little sense I had left when that thing landed on me!"

He held out his hand and took hers. His strength pulled her upright. "Wash your face; you'll feel better. Use the upper basin pool, its good clean water."

Beth made no reply. His offhanded remarks had angered her.

Twenty minutes later she returned. He was right, she did feel better after washing. She had time to think about the incident. *Sam did not place the horrid spider on her – in fact he had removed it.* He had been busy. The camp was picked up and

stored.   The horse was saddled
and ready to go.   He boosted her
up on the horse and led off on
foot, walking at first, and then
he increased to a trot.   The
sunset came and he ran steadily
into the night leading the grey
horse at a steady pace.

Beth clung to the saddle horn
and   could   only   marvel   at   the
endurance of the man.   As the
hours passed, he continued to run
steadily. *Beth wondered silently
what Sam's thoughts were as he
ran without even breathing hard.*

Sam was remembering how he had
been taught as an Apache to run
for days.   Now he open all of his
senses to the desert – he needed
to be aware of any Apaches before
they were aware of him or the
girl.

Slavery of Native Americans had long been a problem in the southwest. Many whites opposed the reservation system because it reduced the number of Indians available for capture and ultimate slavery. In June of 1865, President Andrew Johnson notified all departments to take every means available to suppress the slave trade among the Native Americans. However, it was not until Feb 1867 that an act was passed by Congress to prohibit the practice of Indian slavery, which effectively outlawed the 'system of Peonage' among the Native-Americans. Even with stiff penalties for violations the practice lingered, and continued to be one of the many sources of grievance and poor relations between the Anglos and Apache.

Chapter Five

Sergeant Major Nathan B. MacPherson was standing, just looking out over the desert. He was a big man, standing well over six-four in his stocking feet. His size was imposing. He stood squarely behind a large rock almost as tall as he was; with just his head above the rock. Nathan had reddish bushy hair and freckles covered his exposed arms and face. A square chiseled face-showing evidence of many battles, thickened eyebrows from scars, and his nose no longer straight. His eyes were pale-blue which blended with horizon. He stood still, not moving his head – just his eyes.

Right now the big man didn't feel very big, he felt small, a little speck in a vast country. Also, he was worried: about completing his assigned task, about the cargo in the wagons, but mostly, about his men. Taking out his service binoculars, he again scanned the horizon, then systematically looked at each rock and cacti. There was nothing to see - but he knew they were out there. He could feel it in his gut, years of military experience had given Nathan that sixth sense.

Finally, he lowered his head and glanced back at the ragtag band of thirty men and one young Lieutenant that he was responsible for. There were also six wagons and forty horses and mules. The horses alone would be a treasure to any Native Indians. However, the cargo they carried was even more precious than gold to the Apache - the wagons were full of guns and ammunition. These guns and ammunition were vital supplies needed at Fort Yuma. This was too big to be kept a secret in this lonely country. Any military man with even half a brain had to assume that word of this shipment had been talked about.

Although this was new country for Nathan, he had been in the desert before, while riding with her Majesty's forces in the Sahara and Middle East - yes Nathan knew the deserts. He understood the needs for water, and the endurance of men and animals in this desolate land. That was one of the reasons he had been selected for this job. His Lieutenant was a good Officer who had just graduated from West Point last year - and to McPherson's knowledge the man had never seen battle

"Sergeant Major, just how much longer are we going to just sit here?" Nathan recognized the accented voice of Sergeant Von Chek.

Von Chek was a tall lanky man

with thin a gaunt face, big nose and black hair; he was not a handsome even by a man's standard. He was a fighter with long arms to reach in a pound at most men – McPherson knew he would have to watch him. Well, the man seemed reasonably competent despite his attitude.

McPherson paused before replying. "We'll wait at least until dark. The horses need rest. The men need rest. Post the guard and tell the others to get some sleep. Rotate in three hours."

"Okay, Sergeant Major." The man turned and walked away to follow the big McPherson orders. He went back to watching.

He did not watch the flurry in the camp as Von Chek executed his orders. McPherson removed his pipe and tobacco pouch from his pocket. Slowly and methodically he packed then lit his pipe. This was one of the few pleasures that he permitted himself. As he drew on the pipe he slowly contemplated his defensive position – which he did not like.

McPherson heard a rustling of

movement, he turned to see old man Jock crawling up beside him. Jock Carter was the one man in his little band that was not regular Army. Jock was only a civilian scout, but he knew this territory and the ways of the Apache. Jock was someone who Sergeant Major McPherson and the Lieutenant had to depend on; and over the past weeks McPherson had come to respect.

"They're out there, I can feel it." McPherson commented off hand.

"Sure are, you got good feelin's. Most don't know until it's too late." The old man almost cackled.

"Started out tracking Bedouin raiders in the Sara Desert for the British Army. This is not much different."

"Patches is the shiftiest and nastiest Injuns I ever saw. Spent four years out here hunting gold before the war. Seen a heap of things them devils did. They are the best at hiding in plain sight. Never seen'm until it's too late. But you got the right idea, hold the water and high ground."

"Tell me more about the Apache." McPherson prompted the little man.

"Patches is the best. All the other Injuns do a heap of fightin between themselves. Crow, Blackfoot, even the Comanch keep clear of the Patches. Every time other tribes take on the Patches they get there lunch handed to them. The only thing more dangerous than a Patch is a wounded Patch. I rather go in a bear cave. This is the game they like the best, us hold up with lots of loot."

"So how do we get tactical advantage?" McPherson wondered aloud.

"Our advantage is that they are too few in numbers and lack supplies and ammo. They won't attack unless they are sure of a quick, decisive victory. Their way is to ambush and run - ever one is a natural bushwhacker."

"Yes, the Apache seem to be the lords of the desert. You were here during the war, what went on?"

"Well, when the war started

most of the Soldier boys just saddled up an pushed off for the states. Mostly, them from Reb states went south and Yanks went north. Left a whole passel of empty forts. State militia tried to hold some of the forts and keep the peace. Weren't no use. Then Rebs moved in and claimed New Mexico, set up forts. Then the Jackass in command of the Rebs Colonel named Baylor, ordered the killin of all Patches. He figured to kill all the men and sell women and kids as slaves. Patches don't take to being killed – once kinfolk are killed then they go on a blood vengeance. Slavery ain't sometin they cotton to either. Bunch of Baylor's men caught up with Patches up in Gloreieta Canyon north of here – not many came back. Baylor got relieved."

Jock paused to pull out a plug of tobacco, he bit off a piece and spat, before continuing. "Bunch of California volunteers led by Major Carleton came over to take back the territory – by the time they got here all the Rebs had already had a belly full of Patches so they left without any fighting. Them Union soldier boys set up Fort Lowell and a couple of others; then tried to set up good terms with the Patches. Did not last long Patches like to steal and then some white kills a Patch – that sets it off."

"It seems like the white man and the Indians cannot live together," McPherson commented softly.

"It could have been something if'n they had not kill the big Mescillaro Chief – Mangas Coloradas. He was reportedly shot while escaping from Fort McLane. The official Army report is wrong about what happened."

"They often are, especially when politically motivated. Of course, most relations with Indians involve politics. So what really happened to Coloradas?" McPherson asked.

"Bunch of miners got a hold of the Chief. They wanted to prospect the Gileno country. Told the rest of the Patches that Coloradas' safety depended on their good manners. Must have had more than twenty rifles on the Chief. They just walked off with the Chief. Then they meet up with a bunch of troopers. The troopers took custody of the Chief. They took him to the remains of old Fort McLane. The way I heard' it, the two troopers guarding the Chief tormented the man by placing hot bayonets against the Chiefs feet. When he jumped back they shot him. Wern't no white man sorry to see him dead – most figured he had the blood of hundreds on his hands."

"Seem to be plenty of blame for both sides." McPherson relit his pipe. "So the real question is do we stay here in a good defensive position and wait for them to gather more numbers or move out in the night using the darkness for cover."

"Dark don't bother the Patches much. They's not like the Comanch. Patches just soon fight at night as day. In fact, they likes to sneak up on guards at night and kill-em just for the sport."

"How far to the next water?"

"I'd say it's further than

nearer. If'n we leave before the moon rises, should be able to get there before dawn, even with the heavy wagons. Old Fort Lowell surrounds the next hole."

"There are supposed to be troops garrisoned there. What kind of layout will we find?"

Jock knelt on one knee and used his finger to draw in the sand. "Don't know about no troopers there. Last time I was there it was empty as a banker's heart. A rock jumble to the north and a drop off to the south. Only approach is from east or west. Of course we'll be comin in from the east, anyone up in the rocks can have us easy." Jock drew more figures in the sand. "But, once we get in," He pointed to his crude drawing. "Buildings block both approaches from east and west. Easy to hold the hole."

"Thanks." McPherson puffed on his pipe some more.

McPherson watched as Jock erased his marks in the sand. The old man was not much to look at. He was dressed in full buckskins: pants, shirt, jacket, moccasins, and hat. His hair was thin and what little he had was snow white. Deep lines etched in Jock's face almost contained his eyes, but the brown eyes were alert and alive – missing nothing. Even as big as McPherson was, he would not want to take on this man – he was without a doubt, a fighting man, who had survived many battles.

The sun was getting lower and his sixth sense was not as alarmed as it had been earlier. Maybe some the savages had departed. If so he was sure they could have only had one mission, to find more Apaches and bring them to McPherson's small force.

In an instant he made the final decision. Better to move closer to his objective. More soldiers could make the difference. He tapped his pipe on the heel of his boot – time to talk to the Lieutenant. Make the Apache follow – *'Of course that could be a very dangerous game!'*

****

Sam was awake and heard Laglo coming even before he laid his hand on Sam's shoulder. Laglo touched Sam and gave a squeeze, Sam moved his shoulder slightly to let him know he was awake and ready. This was good – a warrior should always be ready. Laglo, Sam's adopted father motioned for him to follow. Sam almost quivered with excitement – his day had arrived Sam was going on a raid.

Down the path Sam went following in the dark behind Laglo. The horses were ready. Less than a minute later they were mounted and off riding in the early morning before sunrise. It started raining before they had gone more than a mile. Sam tried to remember if he was eleven, twelve or thirteen – he was no longer sure anymore. One thing he did know was that most of the boys his age had already been out on a raid. Maybe it was because he was different – not really born of the people that his father had waited so long to take him. Now he was on his way – now Sam had the opportunity to prove himself – to prove that he had the ability to become a good Apache warrior.

It was not until years later

that Sam came to realize that each and every activity in the Apache way of life was preparation to become a Warrior. Whether they played games, did chores, or hunted - it all trained the boys to become good Apache warriors. What required the most training was the Apache body - superb physical conditioning, stamina and fortitude.

Every young man is required to prove himself on raids. As an apprentice he is expected to learn from his elders and do all the work in camp. Raiding is a way of life among the Apache; this is how we live. Raiders were expected to bring back meat; horses, mules, cattle - It does not matter - all can be eaten. Usually it took at least four raids for a young man to become accepted as a warrior. Sam had already seen what happened to boys who refused or were unable to go on raids. They were held in contempt, ridiculed and some even banished. He knew as a boy who was different, it could be even worse.

The group of raiders rode

steadily and restlessly for two days, always going south. To the south in Mexico was the hated Spanish who had mistreated and killed the Apache for hundreds of years. Now it was only natural to raid in Mexico. Not only was there plenty to take, the Spanish were not nearly as well armed as the Anglos. It was always better to take from those who killed the Apache. Laglo hated the Spanish from Mexico – the scalp hunters had killed his brother many years before.

They stopped after two days at around midnight. It had stopped raining, Sam was exhausted after riding two days in the rain, so he fell asleep immediately. He was up and moved out in the pre-dawn darkness towards a small herd of cattle, about forty head. Sam was one of four Apache boys on foot who got the cattle started and by the time it was daylight Sam and his fellow Apache comrades were already miles away from where the cattle had been.

It took three days for Sam and the others to return with the cattle. The four boys drove the cattle on foot continuously, day and night. No sleep, no food, very little water - Sam did what was expected of an Apache raider.

* * * * * * * *

The night was cool as the light of the morning came on. They could gradually see the surrounding desert. This area was even more desolate than the area of the previous day. A land fragmented and torn - a magnificent land, marred and ancient. The landscape was packed with statuesque stones: carved by storms, flash floods, blistering summer heat and harsh winter cold. The land had seen many people come and go - live and die - seasons ravage and bake the land - everything changed, but the land remained.

Sam was still trotting beside the horse as he had been all night. Beth was exhausted from just riding the horse. She could feel that the horse was exhausted from trying to keep pace with Sam. To Beth, this night had been an endless ordeal, but she had not complained, because now the realization of her alternatives had sunk in.

Somehow, she knew in her mind
that they must have crossed the
border between New Mexico and
Arizona. The border was just a
line on a map; she saw no real
difference from yesterday. In
her eyes, they were equally
desolate. Yet, somehow she
gained solace in the quiet beauty
of the endless horizons.

Suddenly· Sam stopped. He
walked forward a couple paces and
just stood there. Beth waited
while minutes rolled by.

"What are we waiting for?"
Finally, Beth could no longer
contain herself.

"Hush. Be still." Sam spoke
almost in a whisper, holding his
finger up to his lips.

Only then, she noticed he was
holding the horse's mouth. He
waited -five-ten- fifteen –
minutes passed. Beth became
painfully aware of the effort
needed to remain perfectly still.
It was really quite difficult to
be still. Somehow, she felt that
it was very important, so she
endured the passing minutes.

At last, he turned and offered
his hand to help her to dismount.

Once down she became aware of her feet - they were tingling.

"Did you see something," She asked quietly?

"No, but they were there crossing ahead of us. Probably looking for us - trying to cross our trail."

"Apache's?"

"Of course, who else would be out here?"

She sat down on flat rock. She looked at her feet, they look almost as bad as they felt - she began to rub her feet.

"Sure need some shoes for this country," he remarked.

"I should have told you that I needed to stop at the first store and get a new pair." They both laughed.

"Well, let's see if I can help."

He kneeled down and took hold of one foot and started a careful exam.

"I beg your pardon," Beth snapped trying to pull back, but he held on tightly.

"Hold still, you have a thorn or cactus needle."

"I got it out."

"No you didn't."

Sam took out a small knife from under his shirt. It looked razor sharp and it was. Holding it between his thumb and forefinger, he gently probed. She whimpered and moaned when he hit a nerve.

"Keep still - I'm not hurting you."

"It's not your foot."

Sam made no reply. Finally, it came out. He stood and walked around; he returned with two small pieces of a plant, which he started to place on the wound. Beth drew back. "You're not going to put some dirty thing on my foot."

"It's cleaner than your foot," He said with a smile.

"Aren't you going to wash out the wound?" She reached for the canteen.

He blocked her hand gently, "Water is too valuable to waste. Best to keep it dry. This will draw out any poison."

She was doubtful, but she allowed him to place the plant parts on her foot and tie it in place with a piece of cloth. Then he offered the water to Beth. She took it and drank; the water was warm and tasted of alkaline – but to her it now tasted pleasant.

Sam stood and stepped to the horse and pulled his saddlebags off in one swift motion. He pulled out a pair of moccasins, and tossed them to her. "Put these on, they'll work better."

"I don't want to be some squaw woman." She snapped.

"Don't worry," Sam answered her. "We will get you some regular shoes that you can change into when we get back to civilization. At least you won't be crippled when we get there."

Beth reluctantly pulled them on then began lacing up the moccasins.

The first recorded clash between the Spanish and the many groups comprising what we now refer to as Apache was in 1599. The Spanish were immediately impressed by the Apache ability as an individual warrior. The Spanish introduced horses to the region, but prohibited Indians from being taught how to ride. Initially the only use the Apache had for a horse was food, however by 1630 the Apache had stopped eating horses and had become a light Calvary. This mobility made the Apache almost invincible; enabling the Apache to force the Spanish from the area, now called Southern Arizona and New Mexico, by 1660. For the next hundred years, the Spanish were unable to gain any serious foothold or maintain any missions for longer than a few years.

Chapter Six

Beth asked bluntly, "So what is it like to be an Apache?"

"What makes you think I was an Apache?"

"You said you were a captive. You walk like a cat. You know the language. Your knowledge of the savage and this land seems to know no end. Shall I go on?"

Sam paused before making any reply; "You know the Apache don't think of themselves as savages. They are of the people and all others are something else. Actually, looking back, it was a fairly good way of life. Things were simple. There was only good and bad. Right or wrong. It was a hard life but this is a hard land – only the hearty can survive."

"Did you marry an Apache woman?"

"No, I was too young. I was probably twelve when I left the Apache."

So what was it like to be an Apache"?

"I don't know what to say. You can't take off your skin and say what's it like to not have your skin. A person can only be what they are. For a while - I was Apache. Now I'm not."

"I'm sorry; I was just trying to understand. Maybe it's not possible for me to understand. Tell me what life was like among Apaches and then maybe I can understand."

"To begin, you can just say,

they are just folks. They eat, they drink, they play games, they work, they love, they hate, and they have a way of life. Oh, lots of people say that they are savages, and they don't believe in God. But I've seen it, they do believe in God. They just talk to him in a different language using different symbols."

Beth picked up a stick. She slowly drew intrusive lines in the sand while listening to his quiet talk. When he stopped she probed with another question, "So how does marriage work?"

"Very much the same as it does any place else. Young man sees a girl he likes. He goes to her father. And gets permission to court her. Back east a young man should have a job for a future; but Apache that wants to impress potential future father-in-law goes out and steals several horses."

"Steals horses!" Her tone indicated that she was dubious.

"Why sure, Apaches make their living raiding. What better way to show your potential than to steal some good horses."

"Okay, so what happens after the marriage?"

"The young man moves into his wife's village. Her family now becomes his family. He builds her a Go-tah – a house to you. Then they settle down to raise kids."

Beth was silent for a while. "Stealing just doesn't seem right."

"Some call it stealing, to the Apache it's just a way of life. A Raider brings home food. The Raiders have the right to give away the animals they have acquired. According to custom, plunder is divided equally among the members of the camp. Warriors do not eat until after children and women have eaten, and the old been taken care of. Is that so different?"

"No, I guess not."

"So why did you quit being an Apache? Did you run away or were your rescued?"

"I was not rescued. Believe it or not, I liked being an Apache; but that was another lifetime. Let's get some sleep." With that

Sam pulled his hat down.

Beth just looked at his still form. She just could not believe that anyone would like being an Apache. After a bit she slept.

Sam raised his hat and looked carefully at the sleeping form of the girl. What was it about her that evoked memories long gone? – Maybe it was just her questions. He remembered that he most likely would have become an Apache warrior but for his last fateful Apache raid.

****

Into the night they rode, eight warriors and two boys on their third raid. For three days, they traveled going south into the remote Sierra Madre Mountains occupied by the hated Mexicans. Some of the villages were never attacked or raided since they were places where the Apache could trade plunder which was of no use to the Apache. They bypassed the friendly villages and went to the ranchos around Oputo along the Bavispe River. There were always many fat cattle, which could be driven off with a minimum of effort.

They camped by Skeleton Canyon the day before the raid. Two warriors went ahead to scout. Sam got little sleep since he was expected to do most of the work. As night fell the scouts returned and reported the locations of the cattle and a store house of food and weapons.

The plan was simple: the force would be split into three smaller groups. The first group of three would drive off the cattle during the night, while at the same time the second group of three would slip into the storehouse and remove whatever they could. The final group was Sam and another warrior; their part would be to attack on the far side as a diversion, but they would wait until just before daylight, or unless any alarm was sounded.

By midnight, Sam was in place with his new rifle. Laglo had just walked up and had handed Sam his rifle – a rifle that Sam had practiced shooting. Sam told Laglo that he would return it – Laglo waved indicated that it was not necessary – what a grand gift for a young warrior.

Sam had an unobstructed view of

the main ranch house and the
bunkhouse. He had settled there
just after helping to place
tumbleweeds in strategic
locations. Sam then waited
during the long hours of
darkness. Two hours before light
he could smell and hear the
cattle being walked off towards
the north. As the moon came up,
Sam could see the second group of
Apache's going into the
storehouse – they made several
trips.

Suddenly, there was a shot and
a Mexican voice calling out in
Spanish. A man appeared on the
porch and started to shoot at
Laglo; Sam shot sure and true.
The other warrior started
shooting also. Fires started as
the Apache lit the tumbleweeds,
which had been placed next to the
house and on the bridge.

Both Sam and his fellow warrior
moved, reloaded, and shot several
times. The Mexicans were pinned
down in their houses. Sam and
his fellow warrior now went to
work. They needed to keep the
Mexicans busy for as long as
possible. The fires burned out.
The heavy logs of the house and

bridge refused to burn. Whenever someone exposed themselves, Sam or one of the Apache would shoot, just to let them know it was not safe to venture outside.

Sunrise brought a change to the tactical situation. Apparently, there was a camp of vaqueros to the east. Sam heard them coming - time to go. There must have been at least fifteen. Flanked on both sides the Mexicans started shooting. Bullets ripped all around Sam, but they could not locate him. He move steadily back to where the horses were. When he got there, only his was left. The other warrior had already slipped away. Sam was not upset. This was as it should be, Sam was expected to do the same. Sam led his horse through the rocks. He probably should have abandoned the horse, but this was his favorite. He was determined to come back with this horse.

Shots rang out as two of the vaqueros located him. Sam slipped into a thicket of cactus. They were all around looking for him, yet they could not find him. The searchers moved away widening

their search. Sam moved
carefully through the massive
thicket to the other side. He
could see a way out - a bridge
went over the river to the other
side. If he could cross the
bridge, once over, he would be
gone into the open range.

Sam mounted swiftly and rode
boldly towards the bridge. No
one saw him. The horse
hesitated; he did not like the
bridge. Sam urged the horse
ahead at a trot. A quarter of
the way across the bridge it
collapsed! Sam remembered the
terror of falling, then
blackness!

When Sam woke he was racked in
pain and tied to a bed. Both
legs were severely broken - the
bone was sticking out on the left
one.

****

Tatsahdago walked the area
again. This is where his brother
had died. The warrior who had
killed Prumi had waited for hours
using Apache concealment. No
Anglo or Mexican could possess
such skills - yet this was not an
Apache - but it was something

else. *A Spirit, maybe? – 'No,' A Spirit would not have any use for an Anglo woman captive.*

The others waited a respectful distance away. Not just because they did not want to disturb the signs of the struggle, the other Apaches knew that this is where the great warrior Prumi had died. They watch as Tatsahdago walked in the place of death. They were uneasy with the nearness of death. They did not fear the death itself, but the mystery and spirit which surrounds death.

Tatsahdago shook with anger, almost unable to control himself. He now knew what had happened to his beloved brother. He drew out his knife and cut his hand allowing the blood to drip into the sand where Prumi had fallen. Tatsahdago spoke the words of a sworn vengeance. *Now, only his death could keep him from killing the murderer of Prumi – whoever he was, along with the Anglo woman who had betrayed Prumi!*

The word 'Apache' is believed to be a corruption form of the Spanish word 'Zuni apachu' meaning 'enemy.' Probably in deference to the fact that Apache's considered anyone not Apache their enemy. Most of the desert tribes or families of the desert spoke a similar language - Athapasan. The Apache referred to themselves as Dine; meaning "the people."

Chapter Seven

Sam halted. He was uneasy for some reason – it was growing light. Beth was starting to get used to sleeping in the day and traveling in the night.

"Why are we stopped?" She asked in a quietly, almost whispering.

"They came by this way." He pointed off in a direction which meant nothing to Beth. "Here."

Beth straighten up in the saddle and looked around. "I don't see anything." He could hear the fright in her tone, she was thinking Apache.

"Nevertheless, they crossed here. But what is even more significant is that the Army crossed here also. A lot of them with wagons and mules."

"How do you know it's the Army?"

"The Army uses wagons with a specific width wheels. Also they travel in a regulation defensive set up with riders ahead of the wagons and riders behind the wagons. After you have seen it a couple of times it's easy to recognize."

"What do we do?" Beth was unsure what good this information was. The tone of her voice reflected this doubt.

"I think they are heading for what I learned as Diablo Wells. I believe the Army built a fort there. If the Army is there, then it's a better chance to get you back on the trail to your father. If nothing else we are probably safer with more guns around us." Sam pointed to the rocks ahead. "See over there, we'll make a dry camp there then get an early start tonight. If we push hard, we can arrive before the Army gets there."

****

Tatsahdago stood over six feet tall; his physique was one of perfection. He wore typical

leather breaches and a loin
cloth. Flowing dark shoulder
length hair was held in place by
a headband. His chest was bare,
showing rippling muscles up his
abdomen and back. The young men
around the fire were held by his
voice not his physical
appearance.

Tatsahdago spoke in clear and
precise Apache, "You can see they
return after years of other wars.
The Anglos now want to control
the Apache. Already, we have
more Anglos this year than in the
past. They bring cattle and
horses. They kill our people.
We have only one choice, take the
cattle and horses and kill the
Anglos." He stalked back and
forth around the low fire.

Gehad interrupted with an
observation. "The whites want
only the valleys – we have the
mountains. They always get more
horses and cattle. Why not let
some whites remain, then they
will bring more cattle and
horses?"

Tatsahdago turned and glazed at
Gehad, eyes burning with furor.
"No! All must go. Our ancestors
fought the Dakota. We drove them

from this land. So it must be
again. There is too little
water. If they will not leave,
they must die!"

There was no doubt that all of
the men would follow Tatsahdago
when he left the camp – *His
medicine was strong.*

* * * * * * * *

Having two broken legs with
bones sticking out is painful –
even for an Apache who is almost
a warrior. Sam never forgot the
pain. After lying for two days a
doctor of sorts came and set the
legs. Four men held him down
while the Mexican Doctor set the
legs. Throughout the entire
process, Sam never let out a
sound – he would not give them
the satisfaction. Sam's legs
ached badly but the pain
gradually diminished over the
next couple of days. Sam was
left alone except for an old
Mexican man who fed and tended to
his needs.

After a week the Vaqueros all
returned, a strange man was with
them – an Anglo, fair skinned
like Sam. Sam could not
understand what they were saying,

since he only understood certain words in Spanish the language of the enemy of his people. Thinking back he realized that they were deciding what to do with him. The decision became apparent the next day when they came for Sam.

The Anglo man spoke softly to Sam in English, "Boy, it ain't no use to try and get away. You can't run. If you do get away, you'll starve or die of thirst."

Sam still made no reply so he continued talking, he was not sure that he still understood English, it had been years. "I'm Reverend Henry Walters. You are obviously not an Apache, so I'm going to take you back to the states. The Lord has returned you to your own kind."

With that four men cut Sam loose and took him out to a covered wagon. Sam tried to resist but it was no use, he was tied in the back of the wagon. This was the beginning of a long trip; as the Reverend Henry drove along he continued to talk to Sam. The old man rambled on, talking for hours, as they traveled across the northern

Mexico into Texas. Then north-
east across the southern states
before turning north towards New
England - his home was in
Vermont.

The words of English were
strangely familiar. At first
they were nothing, but somehow
Sam slowly started to realize the
meaning. Sam just listened over
the weeks never saying a word.
At night the old man read from
his Bible. Stories of the
ancients, stories of Cain and
Able, Noah and his sons, of David
a man who became King. Then one
day he started reading aloud from
another book - a story that held
Sam's attention - Ivanhoe.

Just sitting at the campfire
one evening, the old man was
reading as usual. Sam was lost
in the story when the old Henry
stopped. He closed the book,
removed his spectacles while
rubbing his eyes. Sam wanted
more, he motioned. But, the old
man was not looking at Sam. Sam
tried to get out the words - when
his mouth opened no words came
out. Sam knew how to talk so he
tried again. "Go --- On ----."
Was all he managed to croak out.

The old man looked up and smiled. He opened the book and continued reading.

****

Sam and Beth arrived at the Fort around midnight. It was obvious that the buildings had long been deserted. Sam had left Beth for over an hour while he scouted the area. Beth was getting used to his little scouting missions, but this time he was gone even longer than usual.

The longer he was gone the more apprehensive she became, as a result, she gasped when he touched her arm from behind. The moon was up so she could see him clearly when she turned.

"Don't do that." Beth smacked him lightly and laughed with relief. "Why were you gone so long?"

"It's a big place with lots of dark areas. Had to run all around to make sure someone was not sitting and waiting like I did to Prumi." Sam extended out his hand with a canteen. "Brought you something."

Beth took the fresh water

gratefully and drank deeply before answering. "Thank you. What did you find?"

"The fort is abandoned. No evidence that anyone has been here in a long time - nether Anglo or Apache." Sam said.

Beth could think of no appropriate reply, so she just nodded.

"Come on, I found a nice place for us." Sam took her hand and led her off into the night. Walking along she realized that she had never before walked with a man holding hands. It felt natural somehow with this man.

He took her to a low building cabin made of stones to one side of the small compound.

Beth looked over the adobe sod hut. "Was this the Commanding Officer's house?"

"No, I think it was originally a storage shed?"

"We have and entire empty fort to pick from, and you want me to stay in the store room!" Beth was almost shrill in her contempt.

Sam just chuckled, "I picked this place to stay because it's the nearest to the water and best defensive place for the two of us."

"Oh?" Was all Beth could reply.

Sam went back and brought the horse. Beth took the blankets and spread them side by side just inside the door opening of the shed. Meanwhile, Sam had cared for the horse.

Beth poked slowly around the cabin. Someone had actually lived in here she realized. There were bowls, cups and tin plates. Then she found a comb, something tangible.

Sam entered saying, "I'll find fresh meat in the morning. We will risk a fire then." He paused and walked to the corner by the fire place then opened what appeared to be a heavy wooden door. He pointed, "There are stairs here going down to an old storage area - probably used for dry goods like potatoes. There's also a small tunnel that goes down to the river. If there is an attack before morning go down there and stay - use the tunnel if necessary."

"You seem to think of everything," Beth replied, as she used the comb to work on her hair. Then she noticed his almost hurt look – she realized that he was really just looking out for her. She reached out suddenly and touched his arm, "Thanks." She tried to give him her best smile, "I'm just not used to all this – I'll try harder to be brave."

Something passed between them before he withdrew his arm. "You're brave enough to survive Pumi. You'll be okay. Let's try and get some sleep."

"Alright but I just have to comb this hair, it's so knotted up, I can't sleep on it."

Sand and knots forced her to work on one section at a time. She had wished again she had her brush; it was not so long ago that she sat and brushed her hair while sitting in front of a nice mirror. Now she was reduced to sitting on the ground using a broken comb next to this very strange man.

He stretched out on his blanket and she settled beside him. His

breathing was slow and easy.
Beth tried to determine if he was
asleep. She lay awake unable to
sleep. She shook, not with cold,
but with energy of anxiety. Beth
moved over next to the man, he
stirred to her touch. His
breathing remained the same. She
snuggled, placing her arms around
his chest. His movements were
unchanged. She laid her head on
his muscular arm. Finally, her
fears faded and she fell asleep.

She awoke alone in the
daylight. She could hear the
familiar sounds of horses and
wagons moving outside - then the
sounds of shots.

The most known of the various sub groups of Apache were called such names as Chiricahuas, White Mountain, and Mescaleros. These names became renowned with the fierceness of the Apache. But lost were many other groups – Janos, Jacomes, Mansos, Sumas, etc. – they either merged with other groups or were absorbed into the land. The fact that most were somewhat nomadic and the old Spanish records are vague and conflicting, which only adds to this mystery. Of course others such as Navajos, Kiowa, Yaqui, Pimas, Mohave and Lipans are related to the Apache, but are usually considered separate Native Americans. No matter what their name, some group of Apache dominated the great American Desert from Texas to California and south far into Mexico for hundreds of years.

Chapter Eight

The Apache came at the soldiers in the morning just before daylight while the shadows were long. Jock was not with them, he had gone ahead to scout – thus there was no one to give the men any warning of danger. The wagons were spread out moving through the night. As they came over the rise, the soldiers could see the old empty fort. Their eyes were looking far, not near – the men could see safety and water. They knew that MacPherson intended a layover that also meant rest.

The Apache had studied their enemy well. Lieutenant Evans fell first along with a Corporal and two privates on point with the Lieutenant. They broke the flank, killing Sergeant Jenkins and four others.

The Apache sensed victory, but then accurate shots came from the fort. Two Apache went down and another crawled into some tumbleweed. The shooter anticipated and three shots came in succession. Big MacPherson had sensed something and had taken shelter in a small rock outcrop and had a good line of fire. He opened fire and managed to put lead into two.

Tatsahdago had been standing on a rock face, watching as his battle plan came apart. Suddenly two shots came in succession by him. He dropped down out of sight. He felt something on his cheek, reaching up, then looking at the blood on his hand. He boiled with anger as he realized a rock chip had cut his face.

The fight broke as fast as it had started.

****

As the soldiers rode into the compound they were startled to see the good looking young woman step out of the small building. She was fussing with her hair, after a bit she managed to get one section out of her eyes; of course the rest was sticking out also. The formation was moving at a walk after a long night. The sight of Beth stopped the entire column.

The big man stopped his horse right in front of her, he removed his hat before speaking. "Good mornin missy. I'm Sergeant Major MacPherson."

"Miss Elizabeth Ridgway."

"Are you alone?"

"No…"

"She is with me," Sam interjected. He had not been there just a moment ago. MacPherson was unsettled by the sudden appearance of the man. *Had he been so intent on the pretty girl that he missed seeing the man?* "Sam Jones."

"Good to meet you both. Are you two alone?"

"Yes," Sam replied. "The San Diego stage was ambushed by Prumi's band. The girl is the sole survivor."

That explained it – more or less. MacPherson took out his pipe. As he started filling the pipe he rumbled, "We found the stage and buried the men. Glad to see the lady got away. Nice Henry you got there – Can I assume that you were our mystery shooter who help break that attack."

"Yes," Sam replied.

"Thanks. We can talk later after I get the men located."

****

Vermont was always beautiful country. Splashed with a rainbow of color from the flowers in spring, green and luscious in the summer, alive with orange when the leaves turn in the autumn, and pure white in the winter. Sam never could figure out which season he liked better, but once he started walking again every season was an adventure in discovery. Never before had he found game in the abundance of Vermont.

It had taken almost two months to travel from Mexico back to Vermont. During that time Sam remembered his name and began to slowly to relearn English.

When Sam and the Reverend arrived it was late fall, before the first snowfall. Normally Sam would have been given a room upstairs but with his invalid condition, the Reverend had Sam placed in a cloak closet just off his library. When Sam was carried into the library he was aghast – never before had he seen so many books, nor would he have believed that there were so many. Reverend Walters had read Ivanhoe to Sam at least twice – now here was a treasure of stories.

Sam asked, "Are you going to read all of these books to me?"

"No, son I cannot. Now that I am home I must attend to my responsibilities. However, there is no reason you cannot read the books yourself."

"I can't read."

"Then you must learn."

"I don't know if I can."

"Son, you already told me how you learned the Apache ways. How to hunt, fish, and trail game. Learning words in a book is no different. The letters are signs which lead to the trail of words - then to the paragraphs and pages which paint the picture in your mind."

That began Sam's formal education. Each afternoon the old man would take time to work with him. First the letters and sounds, then small words, then finally Sam progressed to the more complex, just as any ordinary student would. After a few weeks he started mixing in numbers and the concepts of counting that were part of arithmetic. Since this was Sam's only entertainment, he consumed many books before he was able to venture out.

It was early spring just after the last snow when Sam was able to risk going out. The Reverend had found a pair of crutches for

him during the winter and Sam
learned ever so tediously how to
move around. The Reverend was
surprised at the speed of Sam's
recovery and his ability to
overcome the adversity. Since
the Reverend had never had to
endure even one day being an
Apache he had no idea that just
being an Apache was much more
difficult than learning to walk
again.

With spring, Sam was allowed to
sit on the front porch and read
or work on one of the lessons
which the Reverend had prepared
for him. One day while Sam was
sitting there, several boys about
his age came by.

"So this is the Squaw boy," the
bigger one commented.

"Just sittin there taken
advantage of all the good
people."

Sam did not reply, however, he
was seething inside. They
continued to taunt him. Sam just
sat there in silence. Finally
they grew tired, since Sam did
not offer any reply, they just
went away.

****

It took more than an hour before they spoke again. Sam had watched MacPherson and Sergeant Von Chek direct the soldiers in the placement of the wagons and horses. The fort was located on a small mesa which held the high ground in the area. In the center of the encampment was the natural spring. Every bit of open ground was covered. Wagons were placed on the east and west approaches taking advantage of the rock wall and building to the south and the downhill slope to the north.

Sam was frying a rabbit when MacPherson and Jock approached. Beth was sitting on the short stone wall which branched off from the work shed. Jock sniffed, smelling the rabbit, "Brought some coffee, figured you might be on short rations."

"Thanks," Sam replied pointing to a small pot of boiling water. Neither of the men had a need for further conversation. Sam watched as Jock added the coffee to the water and started brewing the coffee.

MacPherson, on the other hand, was always ready for any

opportunity to speak with someone other than his troopers or Jock here. "Now that we are all settled, would you like to brief me on your situation?"

So Beth launched into her story relating her position as a General's daughter, her travels to California and finally about her abduction. MacPherson and Jock exchanged glances upon hearing about the death of Prumi; *each realized that Sam was a formidable fighter who understood the Apache.* Since she was somewhat embarrassed about her travels alone with Sam, she skipped or glossed over these aspects of her story.

Finally she ran down into silence, MacPherson asked, "Let me get this straight. You were captured by an Apache warrior and Sam here ambushed and killed him."

"Yes," she squeaked a reply.

"A man alone. Never heard of such a thing," Jock hissed.

Jock made a statement as a matter of fact, "Y'all know them Patches is just sittin out there waiten. They is working up to attack us."

"Oh my," Beth said.

"We have food, rifles and ammunition. Guess we are a tempting target." McPherson commented.

Sam removed the rabbit from the pan and started placing two pieces on each of the serving pans. "No doubt, but your force is still too strong for a single family raiding party, it would take an entire clan or gathering to mount a threat."

"Sounds like you know about Patches," Jock replied.

"Enough," Sam replied softly as he passed out the rabbit. He was sorry that he had been so bold to say anything.

"Well, it seems that things are about as bad as they can get in this territory." MacPherson took a bite before continuing. "I got a note from the Fort Yuma Commander. It seems that the Mescaleros and the Navajos have left the reservations. Apparently, drought and bugs have destroyed all of the crops. So most just went away into the mountains from the reservations."

"Reservations!" Jock spat towards the fire, "Just a fancy name for a prison."

"That is certainly true," Sam added. "Penning up a free person is just as cruel as clipping the wings of a bird."

"No matter what we think," MacPherson interjected. "Just as sure as ants find honey - is that the Army is just a branch of the United States government, as such, it is our duty to carry out the directions of our leaders. No matter what we think of the orders."

Sam tossed down his pan. "I for one, am no longer in the Army, and I'll say my opinion whenever I want. The policies of the United States towards any of the Indians have always been appalling."

Jock cackled, "You got that right boy! I sure liked Old Hickory, but he sure hated injuns. Moving all them injuns to the territories ought to have been a crime. But the truth in the buttermilk is that no matter what the government says, the folks out here just got to live with the situation."

MacPherson asked, "So what exactly do you think is the situation?"

Jock rubbed his face then used his hands to brush back his hair before replying. "Heap of sign – an it ain't good. Ther's enough Patchs gathern to give us a real fight. Maybe twenty or twenty-five."

"Closer to thirty-five or forty," Sam added.

Jock looked at Sam, "Seems you know more about Patches than you been letten on."

"Just the usual," Sam replied uncomfortably. He was even sorrier that he had said anything at all.

"A little," Beth was incredulous. "He lived with the Apache as a boy and he speaks the language." Sam just hung his head down.

Neither of the men replied, they just looked at one another. *However, this revelation placed Sam in a new category as far as both men were concerned.* It was an impressive thing to kill a single Apache in combat, but anyone who lived with the Apache knew the Apache.

"I thought a normal raiding party would only be about ten or fifteen?"

When Sam made no reply Jock continued, "That's a fact, but when there's a big prize or they is really mad they get together. I rather face a battalion of regular troops than take on forty Patches."

****

When Jock arrived back, the soldiers were digging to bury their dead. Ten were laid out already, wrapped in blankets. Jock looked at Von Chek, "Only dig five graves, bury e'm two to a hole."

"Damn you old man, you can't give orders here!" The Sergeant's tone was repugnant.

"Why?" came MacPherson voice. Von Chek stopped in his tracks, *he knew that he would be overruled and he did not like it one bit.*

"Don't need to let the Patches know how many they kil't. They won't dig up a grave to count bodies, but they can count graves."

Due to the fierceness of the Apache the Spanish made no attempt to settle the region known today mostly as Arizona during the seventeenth century. The Spanish had explored as far north as Casa Grande, and in fact made a significant silver discovery at Ariaonac (near what today is Arizona/Sorona border)- Huge lumps of silver (*Bolas de plata*). This brought miners into the area during the 1730's. The tremendous lumps of silver were quickly depleted. When no veins were found, the Prospectors soon lost interest.

Chapter Nine

As the sun went down the evening clouds displayed an eerie reddish glow. "I've never seen any sunset like it," Beth muttered.

Jock was standing nearby. "You never will anywhere else. It seems like it's just more out here with the emptiness and reflections off the red rocks of the desert.

It had been a long warm day, and even now in the twilight it was still warm. Already, the temperature was dropping, it would seem chilly. Even when the temperature would drop twenty degrees, it would not really be cool.

"Where is Sam?" Jock asked.

"I don't know," Beth replied. "He took off a couple of hours ago. He wanted to scout around."

"Guess that fits."

"What does that mean?"

"Well, I got to talking with Sergeant MacPherson this afternoon. You may not know girly, but MacPherson served as an Officer during the great conflict. It seems that he knows your Sam Jones - by reputation. He made the connection after your little speech this morning. Have you noticed that Sam wears a pair of Calvary issue trousers with the stripes torn off?"

"Oh sure, Beth said. "Sam said that he had been a Sergeant Major during the war - of course, I did not believe him. All the Sergeant Major's I ever knew were old enough to be my grandfather."

"Better reset your time." Jock coughed and spat tobacco. "MacPherson tells me he was Grant's Chief Scout during the 'Battle of the Wilderness'. Pears young Sam was the favorite of Grant. It was said that Sam could slip in, nap with the rebs, count all their bullets, and be gone before they ever knew he was there. Highly decorated too. Yes Sir. Quite a lad."

****

It took almost three years for Sam to fully heal from the injuries. Even so he knew that he would never be able to run as fast as before. Cold weather now made his knees ache – not hurt just ache. Somehow, Sam became aware that he would feel the effects of such a catastrophic injury for the rest of his days. Some days Sam was able to walk around most of the day. School in Vermont became a real pleasure; once he learned to read. Reading became his only real pleasure during the long recuperation. Sam went through most of Reverend Walters's extensive collection of books, and then started on the local library.

It took four of them – probably just to gather up the nerve. They caught Sam coming out of the side door from the library. Sam was concentrating on the door and the wind while trying to hold on to a pile of books. Then Sam was pushed hard from behind, already somewhat off balance he went down hard since there was two steps to the ground. Sam rolled automatically, which allowed him to miss most of the blows from the kicks. The books were dropped and Sam was up instantly – which seemed to catch them by surprise.

One boy probably the one who had pushed Sam shut the door eliminating one avenue of escape. Two others came running at Sam full tilt intending to knock him off his feet again. Led by the big oaf that taunted Sam with the name 'squaw boy' at every opportunity. Sam caught him in mid stride and flipped him with a rolling hip throw; the big boy's momentum sent him crashing into a hedge. The next one came in fairly fast too, a fast side step, and a kicked in the stomach sent him down, gasping for air.

The last two came together, with the big one talking. "Kicking ain't polite squaw boy." Sam made no response. Both had fists up and came in trying to flank Sam.

Sam kicked out again at the one on the left but it was a feint; the boy dropped his guard so Sam drilled him stiff hand in the throat. Before the fourth could act, Sam kicked again, backwards, catching him square in the chest. The boy landed flat on his back in the mud.

None seemed really ready to get up and resume the fight so Sam bent down and started gathering his books. The first attacker with a red shirt had now gotten up. Sam could see in his eyes that he had lost the courage. His face was as red as his shirt. Blood started to form from the scratch; apparently the bushes had thorns. "This ain't over, squaw boy."

"It's over, nincompoop." Sam stated flatly as he pulled a knife from under his shirt. Their eyes got big, looking at ten inches of steel. "Touch me again and there will be blood."

"You don't scare me." Red shirt was blustering now. But, he was backing down the alley. The others quickly joined him.

That evening when the old man came in he stopped by Sam's chair. "I heard you had a problem today."

"No, not really."

"I'm told that you assaulted

four boys and then threatened them with a knife." The old man was not accusing just looking for facts.

"I threatened them with a knife, but only after they were rude."

"I believe you." He sat in his easy chair reaching for his pipe. "However, when it's the word of four against one most people will believe the four over one."

"You know some of the language of the people. There is a word in English that I have come to learn since living here - there is no word for it in Apache. The word is lie."

"Ask me in Apache what happened. I'll tell you how I defended myself and restrained myself and did not kill them only out of respect to you."

"That will not be necessary, Son."

Finally, Sam realized that he had his trust.

Now that the boys knew that he carried a knife - they never attempted to assault him again. They would shout insults - but only from a distance.

****

It was now fully dark. Both Jock and Beth were startled when Sam materialized from the shadows. Jock was a scout and had been around Indians most of his life. He knew the ways of the Comanche, Creek, Kiowa, and Apache – this young man had all the moves. Jock was good – but he recognized immediately that Sam was better and younger with better reflexes. From his observation Sam had a natural knack for stealth and handling of weapons.

"Well Son." Jock asked, "What's is the situation?"

"Not good we need to pull in and get a tighter defense. We've already lost one of the out guards."

Suddenly, from the darkness there was a scream. Not just a scream but the wrenching of a man in torment. Beth threw her arms around Sam's neck and held tightly. These were the same screams she heard in her dreams – the screams of the men as she was taken away from the stage. "Oh Sam, what is it?" Sam settled down slowly while the girl held to him.

Jock had been looking into the dark, he squatted down. "Our missing guard."

"That's right." Sam confirmed.

Beth looked at Sam, then at Jock. "Can you help the poor man?" She looked at Sam then at Jock, they said nothing, - their faces said everything.

Big MacPherson and Sergeant Von Chek came crawling up to their position. Sergeant Von Chek's face was clouded with anger.

"What's happening?" Big MacPherson asked as a new series of screams pierced the nigh.

Jock spat tobacco. "Pears one of our boys got careless. Sam here wants to pull back."

"What makes him an expert?" Sergeant Von Chek demanded.

"I say so." Jock spat again. "You posted the guards. I'd say you have to take your share of any blame."

Sergeant Von Chek was an angry man, even in the semi-darkness color could be seen. Before anyone could say anymore the man started screaming again in the darkness. Everyone was quiet listening to the cries from the darkness. Minutes ticked by finally they stopped.

"What are the bastards doing to him?" the Sergeant asked wiping his forehead with his bandanna.

Sam cleared his throat before speaking, "They have him tied upside down probably to a cactus with hot coals heating his head. That makes him crazy. He's being skinning slowly; that's why he is in pain. They figure his cries of pain will unnerve us."

Beth surged from Sam's arms and was sick. The men looked away.

MacPherson looked from Sam and Jock. "What troop defense do you think is best?"

"Bring them all up on the Mesa. Defend the Wagons and the water." Jock started to spit but looked at Beth and hesitated.

Jock looked at MacPherson and motioned towards the shack. Line them up in twos along that wall and on the other side in the gully. Disperse the rest under the wagons. Tell em to dig in."

Big MacPherson motioned for the Sergeant to go. He did, crawling off to gather in the remaining men. He got up on his knees.

"Anything else?"

Sam wet his neckerchief and handed it to Beth, she wiped her face. Sam watched Beth as he spoke. "Have the men sleep half between now and say one-thirty; then the other half must sleep. Everyone must be awake and alert once the moon rises. They will attack before dawn." The screams of the man being tortured interrupted. "They will slip in among us in the dark. Be ready with knives and short guns."

MacPherson asked, "How can you be sure?"

"I listened to them make plans, while I was watching them string up your man. Also that's what I would do if I had a group of Apache warriors. Your men are too noisy and talk too much."

With that MacPherson was gone, Jock took off going the other way. Soon the soldiers started taking up positions along the mesa. During this time the man being tortured continued to cry out throughout the night air. There were periods when the man was quiet then he would start again.

Beth sat quietly for a long

time. She drew her blanket up around her shoulders. "How could you live with people who do such despicable things?"

Sam was not sure how to answer without making her mad, so he paused a long moment before responding. "If you recall, I did not actively seek that lifestyle. Now that I have the experience in both worlds I still would not choose to live as an Apache." Sam took out a cigar and placed it between his lips making no effort to light it. "The Apache way of life is doomed, they just don't know it yet. They just do not realize how great the power of the Army is. The Army will defeat them just as sure as they defeated the south and all the other Indian tribes in the east. Just as the Apache defeated the people who lived here before they did. That is the way of the world."

"That does not excuse what is happening out there."

"No, but I've see worse done by our race. Did you ever read about the Scalp hunters, or read about what happened to the prisoners of war in Andersonville, or what Quantrill did? We whites also have people who have committed far greater atrocities - some in the name of God - the Spanish were probably the very worst in their treatment of the Indians. Those Apaches out there are fighting for their survival and the survival of their way of life. What they are doing is just a tactic; that man is dead - just as dead as if he had an arrow shot through his heart."

"That does not make it right."

"No it's not right - making any creature suffer is wrong, far better to be killed outright. Try and shut it out of your mind, if you don't, you will not be able to think straight. Then you will be vulnerable when they come. They are counting on it."

Beth shivered from a scream. "Okay, I'll try."

Sam reached over and patted her hand. "Lay here and get some sleep, I'll stay close by."

They lay down on the blankets, she knew that she could not sleep but there was nothing else to do. This was a time to wait. It was well after midnight when the screams stopped.

There are those who believe that one of the significant factors which led to the acquisition of southern Arizona and New Mexico to the United States through the Treaty of Guadalupe Hidalgo was the Apache. The Spanish had been unable to control and conquer the Apache and the Mexican government had been even less successful. Someone felt it was a good way to get even with the Americans who had invaded Mexico - let the Americans have the Apache and all the headaches that came with them.

Chapter Ten

She did not intend to sleep but she must have. Reaching out to touch the form beside her, she felt something hard. He had placed a saddle under his blanket. Then she realized the moon was up. There was no war screams, just the rush of bodies. A lot of bodies moving - thumps, grunts and stifled whoops of pain. Two revolvers fired on either side of the encampment. Then came a screeching call of a bird. The battle was over.

"Three men dead and five wounded," Jock reported ten minutes later. The little group had gathered around a lean-to next to the storage shed where Sam and Beth had spent their first night in the old fort. Beth was huddled in a corner just listening.

Big MacPherson slumped from the news. "Guess it would have been worse if we had not pulled back." He pulled out his pipe and started packing it.

Jock was more direct. "We can't take another attack like that. I saw Sam there kill one. I drew blood and so did a couple of the others."

"What stopped the attack?" Sergeant Von Chek wanted to know.

Jock chuckled, "It was Sam out in the brush hooten like an Owl."

"What?" Big MacPherson lit his pipe.

"Hooten like an owl." Jock slapped his pant leg and snorted in mirth. "Patches believe owls is bad medicine. They skedadled when they thought an owl was around."

Everyone looked at Sam for a response. "It was a long shot. Had to try something."

"What now?" Sergeant Von Chek voice dripped with blame that more troopers had been killed.

"Before it gets fully light let's get someone up in that clump of rocks with a long rifle. Maybe he can do some damage during the day." Sam pulled out his unlit cigar and motioned to MacPherson who was getting ready to light his pipe. I'm going to slip out and find their horses. If I can get the horses then we have a chance to break out. Some of the younger ones are edgy after the owl. We have the only water for forty miles."

"Could work." Jock smiled. "But its powerful risky. More than likely you'll get your throat cut."

"More than likely." Sam smiled back.

****

Every day there was more and more talk about the coming war. Then after the election of Abraham Lincoln it became accepted as a certainty. Sam had read much of what Mr. Lincoln had been saying. He was a man who made a lot of sense. Then there came the news about Fort Sumter, which brought the calls for raising the Vermont battalion. By now Sam could walk normally and was even running again. In fact, he made it a practice to spend days away in the forest, hunting and fishing. Sam decided that he was probably seventeen or eighteen years old, considered healthy and fit for military service.

One evening while sitting on the porch reading an Army officer arrived at the Reverend's gate. At the time Sam had no idea what his rank was – thinking back later, he realized the man was a second lieutenant in the militia. He was dressed in a new uniform there were creases as he walked up the path after tying his horse to the picket fence.

"Sam, Sam Jones?" The Lieutenant was almost as young as Sam was. He did not even shave yet.

"Yes." Sam did not move, nor stand up as the reverend felt was good manners.

"I'm out speaking to all the men of the area concerning enlistment." He placed one foot on the first step and leaned forward with his hand on the hilt of his sword.

Sam was ready. "Well, sir. I

have been reading about the glorious opportunity we have to free the slaves and preserve the Union."

"That's right, I assume that you are ready to join the cause?"

"No." Sam replied in a no-nonsense tone.

"No!" Sam could see that he was incredulous. Now Sam really looked at him for the first time. The uniform made him look older. The realization hit Sam – this man had never been in combat. Had he been he would have spoken differently. A warrior can always tell another – this man was not. Of course, it would have done me no good to try to explain.

"Frankly, I am opposed to slavery in any form. But, as far as preservation of the Union - I couldn't care less. I cannot think of one thing that the Union has ever done for me."

He looked like Sam had slapped him; in a way Sam decided that he had.

"Young man have you ever thought about anyone else but yourself. You have a reputation for being a loner, never have you socialized

with any of the young people in
town. This might be your best
chance to make friends with the
other young men. The only friend
you seem to have is old Reverend
Henry Walters."

"Friend – that is a word that
carries a lot of weight, you need
to be careful with it. I would
rather have a few really good
friends, than a thousand of the
fair-thee-well kind. As for the
young men of this town – none have
ever made any attempt to make
friends with me especially during
the months I spent healing from my
injuries. All I have ever
received is insults and assaults."

Three weeks later the boys from
Vermont marched off to war without
Sam.

****

"I'll be back as soon as I can,"
with those few words Sam was ready
to go. "Should be back around
sundown. Don't wait dinner." Sam
looked back, Beth was watching.
Then he moved around a rock and
was gone into the desert.

Even though it was still late
winter it was already shaping up
to a hot day. It would be almost

a hundred by mid-day and climb to a stifling heat before sunset. All of the rocks were hot and even the sand was hot. Any plant used for concealment had thorns. Sam disregarded all of the discomforts as he crawled carefully along. This was no time to run into any of the Apache. Sam moved through the invisible Apache lines, between two warriors spaced about two hundred yards apart.

Once clear of them he moved in a long slow motion, swinging south about two miles. It was slow going since he took great care to leave no tracks. Moving from rock to rock or moving only in soft sand, finally he found the trail of the ponies that concealed his trail. Stopping along the way he rubbed sage and cactus on his cloths to cover his scent. It had taken the better part of three hours to move into a position downwind of the make shift Apache corral.

He squatted and watched. It took only a few minutes to locate the guard. However, with a force of this size there had to be another. Finally the other warrior moved, not much but enough. The second warrior was older and more experienced, Sam would have to take him out first. Slow approach taking almost an hour in the heat. Sam was in no hurry, if he had learned anything from the Apache it was persistence and surreptitious movements. The heat of the day burned in making everything hot, especially the rocks and sand. Once in position he waited. The Apache had moved in this direction twice, maybe he would again. Yes, he moved to check on the animals. The Apache was up and moving, Sam could smell him before he felt or heard the man.

Sam surprised him – he was still reaching for his knife when Sam's knife hit the Apache's heart. The Apache was trained well, not to uttered a sound, as you die. Sam cut his throat to ensure that he would stay quiet.

The younger one was even easier. Lack of experience or alertness was his undoing. Sam took time to dump both bodies in an arroyo, before moving in on the horses. Sam could not believe his luck. Two water bags were hanging in the shade. Sam paused, then took a long drink, before he slashed the bags with his knife.

The horses were ready; they had been idle too long. It took only a moment to pick out the lead mount. Sam leaped to its back and started driving the small herd at a walk. Once they were at least a mile he started driving them at a slow lope. He did not want to raise any dust but he wanted to go fast enough that a running Apache could not catch up.

For the better part of three hours he took the Apache mounts in a wide slow circle. Sam halted the mounts in the mid-afternoon heat and loosely looped them together as a string in the Apache way. This allowed the horses to run well apart but kept the herd from being separated. With the lead rope in hand he moved out. He slowed them to a walk as they approached the Fort again. Finally, he stopped and rode carefully up to the crest of a hill and secured the rope to a large cactus. The horses were tired after being moved in the afternoon heat – they would not be going anywhere without a reason. Of course a reason could be water.

He was up wind where they could not smell.

Sam lay in the shade of a cholla cactus for more than an hour. At last he spotted him – an Apache had seen Sam and was slowly moving in for the kill. This was the hard part pretending not to have seen the enemy approach. It was a skill he had worked at over the years, not only as an Apache but also as a Soldier. Sam waited as the sun went lower. This was what he was waiting for, sunset, it would not be long now. Sam moved like he was making ready to leave – that should hurry the stalker.

The desert was stark and waves of heat caused disturbances in the air. There was stillness – Sam was not fooled. A row of scorpions marched along just over the rise. The stalker disturbed a desert bird that fluttered in a cactus. A lizard crawled up and over a rock – it was still too hot for a lizard to move around undisturbed.

The stalker moved around ready to pounce, but Sam was gone. Before he could react to the realization Sam's strong arm was around his windpipe choking off any sounds and there was a burning in his back as the knife plunged upward through a kidney into his heart.

Sam had an opening. He dropped the dead Apache and leaped to the horses. He lunged ahead, pulling the bunch to a full gallop. He caught movement out of the corner of his eye – another Indian was running full tilt to cut Sam and the horses off, his bow was in hand with an arrow notched. Sam drew his gun and fired as he leaned low over the horses' neck. The arrow flew as the running Apache stumbled. Sam fired again and the Apache went down.

Over the hill they went, bursting onto the Fort's mesa. Sam was half expecting to be shot at by the defenders but no one fired at him. Sam slipped off the mount and dropped almost in front of Beth and Jock. Big MacPherson was standing in the door of the shack. The rifle on the hill barked as the soldier shot out into the desert.

"Looks like you done a fine job, boy." Jock commented before spiting. "We still got some chow."

All Sam could do was smile as the tension and excitement of the day eased from his body. He shook his head, "In a while."

"Are you all right?" Beth pointed to the blood on Sam's shirt and vest.

Sam looked down; "It's not my blood."

One of the few Anglos to have a friendship with any Apache was Thomas J. Jeffords. He arrived in Arizona territory in 1862 carrying dispatches from the Army, then supervised the mail deliveries between Fort Bowie and Tucson. He resigned in disgust after fourteen mail riders had been killed; accusing the Army of failing to protect them. In a bold move he made an effort to learn the language and then went into the hills to find the strong hold of Cochise. He rode in alone and turned over his weapons to the Chief while they talked. A white man of such courage impressed Cochise and after several days of visiting the two formed a firm and lasting friendship.

Chapter Eleven

"They're gone." Beth could hear the excited voices outside. As usual, the pallet where Sam had slept was empty. She and Sam had moved back inside the little building. Sam must have been exhausted because he fell asleep immediately, snoring softly. Beth jumped up and went towards the sound of the men's voices while brushing the sand from her dress. She took only the few moments to slip on the moccasins.

Jock, Big MacPherson, and Sergeant Von Chek were standing around the coffee pot. The men turned and looked admiringly at her in the early morning light, she was getting used to the men. She had now come to realize that by taking the time to admire her they were actually paying her a silent compliment.

"Did I hear you say the Apaches are gone?" Beth still could not believe it.

"Yep." Jock almost snorted. "Up and pulled out. Reck'n Sam made'em think they had bad medicine."

"Have you seen Sam?" Beth glanced out at the scenery.

"Right here," Sam replied softly. Somehow he had again appeared while they were looking in the distance.

Sergeant Von Chek jumped being startled. "Hell's bells - why don't you make a little noise when you slip up. I hate cats and sneaky bastards. I think that your still part Apache."

Sam looked at the man and shrugged in indifference to the

man. "The Apache have a saying. Think what you want. You have to live with yourself. Of course, I could care less what you think." Sam shifted his glance to Beth dismissing the man. "Good morning Beth, you look radiant this morning."

The Sergeant moved fast, grabbing Sam's shoulder with one hand, spinning Sam around. "No man talks to me that way..." Sergeant Von Chek looked down and the color drained from his face. Sam had his large knife pressed against the Sergeants shirt – a dot of red appeared.

Big MacPherson called out, "Sergeant go check the horses."

The Sergeant stepped back wavering somewhat. Beads of sweat appeared on his forehead. "I'll just go and check the horses." The Sergeant Von Chek backed around the corner and was gone.

Sam stepped up the coffee pot and poured himself a cup. The knife was gone.

Big MacPherson ignored the incident. "I think we should move out as soon as possible."

Glances of agreement met his

statement. Jock seemed to reply for everyone, "The sooner the better."

"Okay, pass the word saddle up."

After the two men had left Beth turned to Sam, "Was that necessary?"

"What?" Sam acted dumb, but it did not work.

"I hope that display with the Sergeant was not for me. I am already aware of your abilities."

Sam shook his head, "I'm sorry that you'd think that way. I did what was necessary to prevent injury. A man does not become a Sergeant in the Army without being handy with his fists. I did not feel like fighting him this morning, as we have all agreed it's time to move out. So I removed the option of fighting."

"Your actions are brutal."

"Brutal or not, but by making him realize that his actions would result in serious results. I defused the situation."

"It appeared that Sergeant Major MacPherson ended the situation."

"Big Mac just gave the man an easy way out. Just remember Beth the best way to prevent violence is strength and being willing to apply force when necessary to back it up. You will live in peace and be left alone if you remember that."

Beth did not know what to say, he seemed so sure. She changed the subject. "Guess we had better get ready."

Sam finished his coffee and started gathering up the camp utensils. Beth went in and started on the bedrolls.

She was angry with herself, she had reacted based on what she had learned in school. She realized that the teachers in a civilized controlled environment of school were out of touch and that Sam was right. The thin film of civilization was only held together by force and men being willing to fight to keep the peace. Back east, there were police and courts to keep the peace. Even there the police had guns and had to use violence to keep the peace. Out here in the wilderness of the desert, these facts were amplified by the daily tests of survival. Each person has to be ready to enforce justice.

****

When the Vermont battalion left with almost all the young men, everyone in town thought they would be home by fall harvest, or at the latest by Christmas. In fact, all through the summer that was the talk around town. Then the reports started coming back about the terrible battles.

Even with Sam's experience with the Apache, he had never dreamed of battle on such an immense scale. When the Apache fight its tens or twenties; and engagement involving hundreds was the stuff of songs or great tales. No Apache could envision thousands being involved in a battle.

Sam became obsessed with reading the papers and posted news about the war. If what he read was true then thousands were involved. This war was taking on a scale only seen in previous history by notables such as: Napoleon, Genghis Khan, or Julius Caesar. Seven states had seceded originally to form the Confederate States but four other slave states followed after Lincoln called for each state to provide men for the Army.

Sam brought up the causes of the war with his friend and mentor Reverend Henry. Henry explained to Sam that all wars by civilizations such as ours were basically caused by economics. Although, slavery is the issue the fact that the southern states economy was based on slavery, the economic issue became the real threat to the south.

Sam had the natural aversion of any Apache to the thought of being held as a prisoner or slave. Sam developed a growing dread the nation and this American civilization was being torn apart - and nothing would ever again be the same.

So, Sam went fishing or hunting as often as possible. Each trip was longer, each time further and in different directions looking for peace. One day returning from a trip, Sam came across a new enclosure. It was near the next town over. There were hundreds of men gathered. His first thought was that it was a fort. There were towers and walls. Then he realized it was a prison - a prison of war camp for confederate soldiers.

He studied them for a while. They looked just like the rest of us. Finally, a Union soldier came along and told Sam to move along.

It was a place of great evil. Sam was quite willing to leave.

****

Dust and more dust. Even so, Beth was not unhappy. For the first time in days - she felt safe. She was tired of being on the edge. At first when captured, she had been terrified. Then after her rescue, she had been grateful and mad. Sam was just so infuriating, yet likeable. Then during this last siege, she had just been scared. Now she was relieved and safe being on the road traveling back to her father.

Beth and Sam rode side by side on their horses behind the first wagon. She asked herself, did she feel safe because she was in the company of the Army? Many of her girlhood memories of being around the forts always made her feel safe. No, she had felt safe ever since she had met Sam. If only he could see things her way.

She rubbed her arm where a thorn had cut her. She needed to find the plant that Sam had used before. Her moccasins had protected her legs and feet on more than one occasion. She rubbed her arm again and realized how lucky she was that he had insisted on the apache footwear.

Sam stated flatly that this was beautiful country. Even her father's letters made comments how she would enjoy the vast views of the west. Her opinions and attitude was shaped by one of her instructors at the academy, Miss. Lucy Smith, who had stated that; 'The Great American Desert was a desolate and God-forsaken place.' Miss. Smith further expounded; 'that every insect stings, every plant has thorns, poisonous snakes, lizards and spiders lie in every crevice. Nothing travels in the desert unless it is a predator – whether savage man or beast.' Beth now realized that Miss. Smith was only correct up to a point, and that Miss. Smith had preconceived misconceptions like so many who lived back East.

Now Sam had provided new lessons on this dry land. Many species of cactus can be handled and many contain the life giving water. Most cactus also have flowers some quite beautiful. Plants are medicines in many cases even if they cannot be eaten. While other like sage, make game hens taste better. Last night she had just eaten what Sam had prepared. When she was finished, she asked where he had gotten a chicken – he just smiled and told her it was snake.

She now understood what Sam meant the other day after she had commented on how strange the desert was. He said, "It's only strange because you are not used to it. No matter where you go, nature is the same. Everything has a place and a purpose. If it ceases to have a place or purpose it ceases to exist."

Beth pulled down the bandana that she was wearing to cover her mouth, "Sam, why would they leave? Not like Jock says, just bad medicine."

Sam looked over "It could be, but in all likelihood they just decided the price was too high. Apaches don't like to lose men. Warriors won't support a fight that is too costly unless it is a vengeance thing."

"Doesn't the Chief just give orders like a General?"

"No the Apache are a free people. The word Chief is an English and Spanish word, there is no Apache word for Chief. Leaders among the Apache are usually elders of small bands and any authority they might have comes only from persuasion and personal prestige. Each individual warrior is absolutely independent and free to come and go as they wish. Believe me, they guard their freedom and independence, although they don't use words like freedom."

"So they may come back."

"It's possible. I have a feeling we are being watched."

****

Tatsahdago stood watching as the column of wagons moved slowly across the desert. Over a mile away, standing by a great cacti, Tatsahdago knew that no one looking could see him since only his head was exposed. He stood motionless for over an hour until the wagons were out of sight.

He watched carefully the two

riders between the first and second wagon, one was the woman Prumi had taken, and the other was the ghost. Nevertheless, the ghost was a man that was clear. A ghost could not be killed – but a man could. Yes, he would kill the ghost man and keep the woman.

Apache first came in contact with Anglo-Americans during the 1820's. The Apache found the Americans, unlike the Spanish they were honest and truthful. The Apache were impressed also with the superior weapons and fighting ability of the Americans. Most of these early contacts had good outcomes; Chief Juan Jose made a treaty with the miners and traded with the Americans. If the Americans had continued to build on this good foundation, it is thought that the troubles and conflict of the late 1800's would have been avoided.

Chapter Twelve

Two days later found the small band of travelers in Gila Valley. Here the terrain was sandy and dry washes. The mounted soldiers had to continuously change direction to follow a path that the wagons could pass. Even so, there were problems in this rough terrain. It was rock, lava rock which was sharp and jagged. Wheels broke and had to be repaired which also slowed them.

Jock was almost always gone; he ranged out ahead scouting the best trails. Occasionally Sam would go with Jock, but for the most part he remained at Beth's side. They rode side by side for long hours, rarely talking, sometimes just because Sam was a quiet guy, but other times because it was practical. Any wind in the desert brought air born sand, if you were talking you got a mouth full of sand.

It was late afternoon when they got to the river. It was not much, but it was water. Sam did not particularly like the wagon crossing point and he mentioned it to Sergeant Von Chek. Sergeant Von Chek told Sam to mind his own business. So Sam and Beth rode a little further upstream and crossed with ease. Once on the other side they rode back down to watch. The first wagon was already stuck about a third of the way across. Von Chek was shouting and cussing. They dismounted and sat in the shade of a cottonwood tree watching the progress.

"You should have gone to the Sergeant Major," Beth stated.

"Why? The Sergeant has to learn. If I run to the Sergeant Major every time I disagree with Von Chek, I'd spend all my time talking with the Sergeant Major.

Not only that, Von Chek was right it was none of my business. I'm not in the Army anymore nor do I have any intention of being in the Army again."

Now the soldiers had stopped floundering. They had unhitched a team from another wagon and with the additional horses were bringing out to the wagon caught in the river.

The first wagon with two teams was making a slow approach to the shore. Jock rode up looking over the operation. He rode over to where Sam and Beth were seated. He spoke after spitting tobacco, "I can see that you two are the only ones with any sense." Sam just smiled so Jock continued, "What lame brain decided to cross here?"

Beth started to reply but Sam held her arm. "It was an Army decision."

Jock just snorted and plunged down the bank and into the river. He went over and talked with Von Chek. He turned his horse and came back muttering to himself – *he obviously was not happy with the exchange that he had with the*

Sergeant.

Jock swung down and paused as he walked past Sam's horse. He tossed some words at Sam, "How's about letting me take a gander at your fancy rifle?"

"Sure," Sam called back

Jock was already pulling rawhide strings that Sam used to tie the rifle to the saddle in a makeshift boot holster. Jock walked up and squatted while studying the gun carefully. "Heard' about these Henrys. Guess them Patches thought you was four or five men when you cut loose with this thing the other morning."

Sam pointed to the underside, "See the secondary barrel? That's where the rounds are stored. There is a spring in there that feeds the magazine each time the lever is cocked. It holds fifteen and with one in the chamber that's sixteen."

Jock jacked the lever open and a metal jacketed cartridge ejected, he scooped it up and looked it over carefully. "Have me a Sharps rifle breach loader back at Fort Yuma – good gun for hunting big game. As you can see the Army is partial to them Spencer's. They's good guns too. But this looks like something else. These cartridges - these will be the wave of the future. About time we got rid of the cap and ball. What'd you pay for a gun like this?"

"Didn't, it's a gift - you can see the US stamp on the stock. An Officer I rode with let me keep it when I got out. I've been told that these go for fifty dollars."

"Lordy be! Fifty Dollars! That's almost two months pay. Ain't no ordinary Officer gonna give a gun like this away."

"Okay, you got me - it was a General."

Jock stood, "Yellow Boy - that what these guns are called. You get tired of it and I'll take it off your hands. It's got a good feel and balance."

"Not a chance." Sam watched as Jock opened the lever again and reloaded. He closed the breach and eased down the trigger.

"You'll have to let me shoot it sometime." He walked back over to Sam's horse and put the gun away.

"You can shoot it now if you

want," Sam replied.

"Nah; I'd better get back to helpin the Army. Want to help?"

"Not particularly." Sam replied.

"Don't blame you." He mounted and went down towards the wagons that had already been pulled across.

After Jock was gone Beth wondered aloud, "So you are going to California to start a ranch. Why California?"

"I was there once. The weather is the best in the entire United States and what I remember of the country, it is excellent for growing citrus and cattle."

Beth looked around, "I was under the impression that California was much like this except in the mountains where they found the gold."

"No, Oh there is desert much like this but there is also plains, great valleys much like the great plains you crossed, and the coast line is as long as the east coast from New Jersey to Florida. It's a big place with room to grow. It's also far enough away from Vermont and the war as I can get."

"So why did you not take the northern route from Independence?"

"I probably should have, but I was familiar with this part of the country. Maybe I just wanted to see if there were any changes. Anyway, if I had I would not have been here to help you."

Beth flushed, "I'm grateful. I am certainly glad we met."

"Miss Ridgway, I also glad to have met you. This is probably the only circumstances that I would have ever been able to have met you or have been able to enjoy your company."

This left each in an awkward pause neither being able to continue. So they watched for a while in silence.

Finally, Beth asked, "So when were you in California?"

Now it was Sam's turn to be uncomfortable, at last he answered. "It was before the war while I was still living with the Apache."

"Oh," came her soft reply drawing the obvious conclusion.

****

Sam rode in a small group mostly

composed of boys. Boys who were not considered warriors, but needed a long excursion as part of their Apache apprenticeship. There were two objectives in this trip, first to expose the future warrior Apache to the desert west of the Gila. This was the territory of the Navajo who roamed between the Gila and the Colorado rivers and the Mojave who controlled the desert west of the Colorado.

Laglo knew one of the great warriors' among the Mojave, Magano. In fact, Magano had married Laglo's older sister. Laglo told the story how Magano came to Laglo's father with ten good horses to bargain with Laglo's father. Each and every one fine quality and broken. This was a marriage of elite families between two peoples, intended to make stronger bonds between allies. This allowed Laglo to ride in comparative safety throughout Mojave areas.

The ride into California took about three days of hard riding and once they arrived at Magano's home camp they were greeted as welcome guests. A hunt was formed and the boys were included. A raid on a Mexican rancho north of San Diego was planned. A hard night of riding through Borrego Springs then up and over the mountains; then down to the coast. They stood on a bluff looking out over the vast Pacific Ocean that extended over the horizon. Laglo explained to the boys that this was the endless water. But, the water was no good – it was not for drinking. Laglo led the group down to the beach; then he told each of the boys to taste the water. The boys immediately spat out the brine water.

"What is beyond?" Sam asked Laglo. Laglo was pleased that his adopted son had asked such a great question.

"It is the unknown realm of spirits. It is where all of the people came from."

With that simple explanation the question was answered, and we left the ocean. Only years later did Sam's reading lead him to learn that there were several oceans and many other civilizations that lay beyond the vast horizon. But at the time it was enough and actually Laglo was not really incorrect.

That night they raided a Mexican rancho. The Apache and Mojave came away with more than fifty horses and thirty beef cattle. The horses and cattle were split with the Mojave's and the Apache drove their spoils back across the desert. They had been gone more than three weeks but the results were worth the trip. Even today Sam remembered the landmarks and route they took. Beth and Sam had used the same spot to cross that Laglo had used to cross the Gila River many years before.

****

Everything was a mess by the time the crossing had been completed. Camp was made and the boys set about to clean and dry everything. It took hours to get straighten up, chores done, all men and animals fed, and finally settled down for the night.

It was near dawn when Sam woke Beth. "They're here," he whispered in a husky voice. He had leaned down close talking softly right in her ear; he smelled funny, like the bushes. He rubbed something on her arms then on her legs. She wanted to protest the indignity but she was too frightened. His words had gone all the way to the bones. She broke out in a sweat of fear of the Apache.

He pulled her gently. He was crawling so she did too. Something moved and she heard a thump. Then he was beside her again. They crawled into bushes. Some of the brush caught her dress; his hands drifted over her body. He was unsnagging her dress from the thorns and branches. In any other circumstances she would have protested, it was improper. Yet somehow in this situation, it seemed appropriate. She felt reassured by his presence and the gentle strokes of his hands.

Then his hand found her shoulder and stopped her forward progress. He leaned his mouth against her ear. "Stay, take this, shake it if someone comes." Something slick and strange – like an arm was placed in her hands. She tried to release it but his hand closed over hers. "Hang on, it's just a dead rattler." He shook her hand and a buzzing noise enveloped them. "It can't hurt you and it will make anyone coming close move real careful. I'm going back, you wait here - stay quiet as possible, rattle if you hear something."

His body had been lying almost over top of her. Now he slid down and leaving her alone in the darkness. She could still feel the warmth of his body and the feel of his hands.

* * * * * * * *

The Apache was young but he was strong and he knew he was able. He had been told to find the Anglos and come back, but he could smell the woman. He could not resist the temptation. Even so he was careful; there had been talk about an Anglo who fought like an Apache. It could not be true but it was best to be careful. It took almost a half an hour to locate her in the tall underbrush; she had tried to hide her scent with sage - that was an Apache child's trick. She was quiet, but quiet for an Anglo woman was not quiet for an Apache. He located the sleeping forms of the men - they all seemed to be there. Finally, he located the Anglo man, he was not as good as he thought he was - first the woman. The young warrior moved around away from the man, then into the thicket. Then he heard the rattle. She did not know how to make the sound of the snake. This would be a mistake that she would never recover from he decided. He moved again along the soft sand where the man had tried to remove his past trail. He heard the woman move again, she had become impatient - no Apache woman would make that mistake.

He waited, then moved. Now he could see her just sitting in the small opening. Her scent was even stronger now. He moved forward on his belly in the sand wiggling like a snake, then the pain leaped into his chest from below. He started to lift up his body but he could not. As he looked down the hand from under the sand pulled the knife out and then plunged in again this time deeper striking his heart.

Beth heard the thud as the body of the Apache was tossed over and Sam came out of the ground. She gave a small gasp and Sam place his arm around her shoulder. "It's over," Sam said softly.

She shook but settled down with
his arm around her. "Thanks,
again" was all she could get out.

By the late 1830's Apache raids reduced the population in northern Mexico from about seven thousand, to less than fifteen hundred. Spanish presidio troops were ineffective against the superior Apaches; since they were poorly provisioned, often underpaid and many were criminals sentenced to the Army rather than prison. The Mexicans of Sonora and Chihuahua felt obliged to use other means to protect themselves. It was decided to wage a war of extermination against the Apache. A bounty of 100 pesos was offered for the Scalp of any Warrior over fourteen. Later bounties of 50 pesos were paid for women and 25 for children. Thus was born the horrendous trade of "Scalp-Hunters."

Chapter Thirteen

"Never seed nothing like it," Jock was kneeling down by the fire. "The kid buried himself in the ground then just kilt that Patch when he crawled over top."

Several of the men just shook their heads in disbelief and awe. But Sergeant Von Chek was not pleased. "You mean he placed the General's daughter out there like bait in a trap. The man should be whipped."

There were murmurs of doubt. "Shut up," Jock shot back. It was too late Beth's head came up, she flushed with embarrassment then anger as the words took effect. She wanted to lash out at Sam, but he was absent – out scouting. The wind whipped around her as she stood looking around. She looked up at the sky as did some of the others. This morning there was no sun just a gray overcast. Now the wind.

Sergeant Major MacPherson and Sam were walking together approaching the small fire. "Jock, how long do you figure we have?"

"Meby an hour or two. But no more'an that."

Beth had walked to Sam with every intention of giving him a piece of her mind, but now she hesitated. There was something else. "Sam what is he talking about?"

"Storm coming – going to be bad. See the clouds over to the east. It's been raining in the high country during the night."

"So?" Beth responded.

Sam explained as matter of fact,

"So when it rains in the mountains, the river we just crossed will get big. This area where we are standing will be underwater in a few hours."

"How do you know this?"

"See the trees, how they grow leaning over? The river bed is low now and even dry sometimes during the summer. But in just a few hours the river will be a mile wide and fierce as any you have seen."

"Oh!" Was all she could think to say.

Now Jock continued, "That's not the worst of it. It probably ain't a-gonna rain here, we'll just get the river flood. But the wind will be whipping up somethin' fierce."

With that, everybody pitched in without the usual griping or petty arguments. Beth noted as she gathered her few beleaguered things that the group could work together like a well-oiled machine. It helped to have the proper motivation and goal. Now there were few wasted motions as she watched the men attach the harnesses to the mules, then the mules were linked together first as teams, then the teams were backed together into position, then connected to the wagon tongue. The mules must have sensed the urgency of the men and for a change offered little resistance. Once all the wagons were ready, they moved out to the southwest.

Even though they only had to move a couple of miles to high ground - it was grueling backbreaking work - hard on the livestock as well as the men. There was no trail here across the seemingly flat volcanic ground. Jock and Sam rode ahead scouting out the easiest path, each riding back to direct the wagons. They were forced to cross back and forth to avoid breaks where the wagons could not cross. Sharp thorny tough cactus grew knee high. As the wind whipped up and horses shied off they came in contact with the thorns of the plants - this entangled the men trying to keep them free. Soon many of the men had bleeding spots from contact with thorns or sharp rocks. Finally, what Sam and Jock were looking for came into sight -

a point of rock jutted up from the level plain several hundred feet into the air. The entire clump was only a mile around. The livestock was moved into a small opening that shielded them from the blowing sand.

Sam pulled Beth from her horse and shoved her under a wagon with a blanket. He was back a few minutes later with a piece of canvas that he pulled over the both of them. They lay there together for hours as the wind howled and screamed with ferocity. They could not talk above the din and finally Beth drifted off to sleep.

When she awoke the wind had stopped. Sam had thrown off the canvas cover bathing them with fresh cool air of the night. It was refreshing after the stuffy confinement. Beth looked up clouds covered the stars. It was a dark night and without a fire the night was even darker. A match struck in the distance and she could see the brief outline of Big MacPherson as he lit his pipe. All around other uncovered and just sat there.

Beth said softly to Sam, "Will

there be more?"

"No Beth, everything is fine, the storm is over, and we have survived."

Beth's breath was heavy with relief. "I don't think I have ever been out in such violent elements."

****

Sam remembered back to another storm of much more violent elements, then with the addition of violent men – a storm that changed his entire life. They said that the storm was the remnants of a hurricane that had started out over the ocean down by Africa. Never the less it still packed a wallop by the time he came ashore in New England. More than ten inches of rain in a morning and then the wind came blowing hard enough to knock down the shanty houses. Then it increased in intensity and took the roofs of others which were thought to be built strongly.

The Reverend had some premonition of what was coming. He had got Sam up early and together they had closed all the shutters and had even nailed shut the ones that did not lock shut. They had filled buckets from the well and filled spare water barrels. So they were prepared when the storm came.

After the rain and hours of deafening wind there was a lull. A knock at the back door and a man with five kids, actually only the boy was a kid the girls were teenagers. The Reverend let them into the warm kitchen. All were soaked and shivering.

"Blankets." The old man ordered.

Sam ran to the upstairs hall and gathered a pile of blankets and towels. The young boy had followed and helped Sam carry them back downstairs.

The man was talking when Sam came back into the room. "Got to go back, could not find my misses or this boy's folks."

The Reverend stood, "Sam, get these kids dry and something to eat. We'll be back soon."

Sam had always done what the old man asked without question; but now Sam knew he was wrong. "Sir, it would be better if I go. You know I move better in the dark than you. I'll find them."

The old man knew immediately that Sam was right. "Okay."

The man protested, "I don't need your Indian boy."

Sam had never seen the old man so mad, his face got red and he puffed out. "You fool! Sam here is no more an Indian than you or I, but with the experience he has been through, he is almost part bloodhound. Be grateful for his offer to help."

The man was downcast from his verbal beating. "All right, let's go."

Out Sam and the man went into the night. The man had a lamp on the back porch that took two tries to light. The streets were flowing mud, trees had been knocked down and no street lamps were illuminated. Everywhere there was devastation and ruin. When they got down to the main street it was flowing like a river. The water was waist deep on Sam and up to the thighs on the man, and it was ice cold.

Finally, they stopped, the man pointed the lamp towards what was left of a house. The roof was mostly gone and water was up almost to the level of the windows on the first floor. With the front door open it was a sure bet that the house was flooded. They moved forward together against the current. "Where do you think she might be?" Sam had to shout above the wind and the beginning of the next round of rain.

"Upstairs where the roof is gone." He pointed with the light.

Inside the house was even worse than outside. The entire back of the house was off and the river had surged in. The stairs, the front hall, and parlor were still intact with furniture floating in the muddy waters. Up the stairs they went then into the devastation. At the end of the hall a large timber blocked the door.

"I could not move it by myself," he explained shouting over the wind. "Have to get inside." He put his shoulder to the massive beam but it did not budge. Sam leaned his shoulder with the man to no effect.

"This is not going to work." Sam shouted back while looking up.

He jumped up and caught a rafter board and heave himself up smoothly vaulting up to the next beam. Then in one quick motion he was on his feet and walking along the beam out into the rain and open sky.

He found her lying next to the door, unconscious but still breathing. Sam heaved her up over his shoulder and climbed backup retracing his steps. The man was where he had left him, it was simple just to lower the woman down to him. "Sally, Sally." He cried her name to no avail.

"We got to get out of here," Sam shouted. He just nodded yes in response – it was too hard to talk above the sound of the storm.

Together they lifted the inert dead weight of the woman. As they came down the stairs Sam grabbed a plank floating. Carefully they placed the woman on it, then proceeded across the area that had once been a street - one on each side to hold her. Rain whipped and lashed at them – the water was freezing cold - Sam's legs were numb after a while, but finally they reached the house.

The woman, Sally, woke up half an hour after getting inside out of the elements. Sam was leaning by the sink pump; the man stood and hugged his kids then walked over and shook Sam's hand. "If ever there's anything…" he could not finish.

"Forget it," Sam replied. The man could only grip his shoulder – Sam understood.

By the next morning the river was already receding and the family insisted on returning to their home. Sam went along and helped the boys to rig a tarp over the roof. By the time he left late in the evening the family was moved into the upper floors and had salvaged little remained of their personal items.

* * * * * * *

They had lost two mules, and Private Conrad had a problem that he was trying to resolve. Apparently he had developed a problem with his bowels, so while they had been trapped under the blowing wind, he had been forced to relieve himself. All the men felt sorry for him, but he reeked and no one could stand to be near him.

Sam and Big MacPherson were standing watching the men digging a couple of wagons from the sand drifts, when Jock came wandering up, "Going scouting," he announced. "Going to take young Conrad with me – back down to the river. If'in I don't, no one's gonna want to be in the same camp or even ride with us."

Both men chuckled, and Big MacPherson told him, "Go ahead – I would guess the Apache would be able to smell him for fifty miles." Then he added on a more serious note, "Try and not get killed, we need every gun. I don't think we are going to be safe until we get to Fort Yuma."

"Seems so," Jock replied while scratching himself in places that polite folks normally did only when alone. "It is kinda curious that they keep following, especially after losing – most Patches would figure it's bad medicine."

Sam cleared his throat before speaking. "I've been giving it some thought. Even though the wagons, food and ammo is a prize beyond belief. I think they're after something even more valuable -- Me and the Girl."

Jock continued to scratch and MacPherson puffed on his pipe; then looked at Sam inquisitively waiting for him to explain. "Before we met up I told you about killing an Apache to get Beth back. I knew that Apache and he had a brother who was only a year or so older. I think that Tatsahdago is the one following – and he is on a vengeance trail."

"That would explain it," Jock retorted.

Sergeant Von Chek had apparently walked up behind the men during the conversation. He responded with anger over the revelation. "You mean all them men died just to protect this man – I say let's toss him out and let him fend for himself." He looked at Sam hard. "It's not just me – none of the men like you."

Sam just looked blankly at Von Chek. Big MacPherson drew himself erect. The man was imposing – he glared at Von Chek before speaking. "I'll hear no more talk like that. Sergeant, Mr. Jones here has proven himself invaluable and I'd never consider casting him out as you have suggested. Although alone, I'm sure he would stand a better chance of survival than with us. You have forgotten that he probably saved your hide; and being inconsiderate I'm sure you forgot to thank him. Why don't you get back to those wagons and see what you can do to get them free."

As Big MacPherson had been speaking Sergeant Von Chek had been getting redder and redder. He was flushed with anger but said nothing. He glared back at Sergeant Major MacPherson and then turned on his heels and walked back to the other men.

Jock looked at Sam, "Sure hope you don't have to kill Von Chek. Right now we need every man. Von Chek was a bereaved Second Lieutenant in the war. Guess he just hasn't taken to being set back down."

"Hell," Big MacPherson snorted; "I was a bereaved Captain but none of that cuts anything out here. He has to learn that, if he doesn't then I'll be forced to deal with him. I just hope he does not get himself killed, or gets any more of the men killed."

Sam was embarrassed so he changed the subject. "Should we assume that the trail between here and Yuma is good going following the river"?

Jock nodded, "You bet, and downhill most of the way with good grass this time of the year."

"Right now our trail is gone, but if we follow the trail, they will pick us up right away. It has been a long time since I've been here. If you was thinking like an Apache where would be the best place for an ambush?"

"There are some rocky hills before we get to Yuma. Lots of places for a good ambush."

Jock just confirmed what Sam was thinking. "Guess you and me, Jock, will just have to ambush the Apache, before they can ambush us."

Mangas Coloradas was one of the most influential and admired of the Meimbrenos Apaches during the 1830's and 40's. Described as a large, powerful man, he was considered a statesman as well. Like the medieval kings, he arranged for diplomatic marriages of his attractive daughters. Thus he was able to ask Cochise, leader of the Chiricaha, and even the Navajo to join him in battle. Coloradas made a mistake trying to deal with miners in the late 1837, after agreeing to show the miners the location abundant with the yellow gold they sought. For some reason the miners decided that Coloradas might lead them into a trap. Next time he came to their camp the miners captured him and tied him to a tree, and whipped him severely. This was a serious mistake - Coloradas spent the rest of his life avenging the humiliation. Many a lone miner died slowly head down over a fire or staked in an anthill to atone for the scars left on his back.

Chapter Fourteen

She was standing by a wagon, leaning, looking out over the vast desolate landscape. The wind was still blowing trailing wisps of hair and had put color in her face. Jock was observing this raw natural beauty. If only he was twenty or thirty years younger, he immediately put such thoughts from his mind and looked at the girl who could be his daughter. He crunched the sand intentionally, she turned; he could see disappointment in her face, he was not the one she expected.

Beth smiled, "Oh, Jock, these men make Sam seem so mean."

"Fools," Jock snorted. "Don't listen to men who know nothing. Were you listening to that last chat?"

"Yes, well uh," she stopped and composed herself. "I guess I expected everything out here to be different, but not this different."

The old man put his arm around her shoulder and gave her a squeeze of reassurance. "Sure it's different, but folks is folks. Even the Patches is folks in their own way. Believe me it ain't every young lady who gets kidnapped and rescued by the handsome brave ex-soldier. Just think what a glorious story you will have to tell your grandchildren."

"Well, it's confusing, everyone

trying to kill each other. For what? This burned out desert - vengeance? Back east it's civilized."

"It ain't all that civilized. My folks fought the Creeks till 'Andy by God Jackson' went out with an Army and put a stop to all the killin'. No, we are moving to tame a continent and there's gonna be casualties. The real trick is not to be one of them."

"That is, more or less what Sam was telling me, but I was not sure whether to believe him."

"You can believe him girl. I got me a reputation for being a good judge of men and horseflesh. One is about the same as the other." He grinned showing his tobacco-stained teeth. "I got a good feeling about young Sam there. Stick with him and you are likely as not to be okay."

"Still, I guess I am reluctant. I really do not know Sam. I guess it's part of the Army life, you do not really get to know people."

"Don't worry that's all part of life. In another lifetime I was married - all the growing and learnin' about one another is part of the venture through life. If you think you got the real thing, grab it – cause it might not come around again." Jock stopped and looked around like a hawk. Then he spit a stream of tobacco juice on an unsuspecting lizard. The lizard promptly scurried away.

Beth pretended not to notice the crude action. When Jock returned his attention to her she mused, "Still I cannot help wondering why he went and joined the Army? He obviously had no allegiance to either side."

Jock replied, "I heard one of the men ask him that question the other day. An all he said was, 'Well it seemed like the thing to do at the time'."

****

The storm had passed and the sun was coming out when Sam returned to the reverend's house, after getting the family back somewhat in to their house – he knew immediately that something was wrong. Then he heard what he had felt; moving quietly now through the house, he could hear muted voices in the kitchen – none were familiar.

He opened the door and just looked on the scene. There were three men in the process of ransacking through the cabinets and shelves. Dishes and pots were scattered, apples were rolling around, and the place was in complete disarray, as he had never seen it. One step forward, then he could see the prone figure of Reverend Henry Walters on the floor – one look was all it took. He knew the man he had come to respect and love was dead!

One bearded man held a piece of cheese and was in the process of cutting off a chunk when he noticed Sam.

"What you looking at, boy?" the bearded man with the cheese asked.

Sam stood mute, carefully appraising the scene. The bearded man smelled, in fact he could smell them all – now, for the first time he understood the smell of evil. It was not that they were unkempt, dirty and had not bathed in a month of Sunday's. The men were evil and reeked of the stench of evil. His anger was building by the moment. The other men stopped and looked, Sam took a long second to observe – the tall one had a pistol in his belt, the grubby little bulky one had an officer's cutlass. He knew the cutlass was what had been used on the unarmed Henry.

The man with the cheese spoke again, "Boy, you live here?" Now Sam shook himself free of all emotions – time to grieve later. The man continued talking, "What's the matter, boy, cat got your tongue? Boy, answer me when..."

The man never finished his sentence as Sam sprang to action. He vaulted over the table taking the man with his feet into his chest. Down he went, the man with the cutlass sprang to action, but the problem with a sword is that it must be drawn from the scabbard and you need room to swing it. Sam gave the man no room to get it into action, he clamped his hand over the arm trying to withdraw the weapon and thrust forward with his knife, plunging it into the bulky man's heart. As Sam withdrew the bulky mans shocked expression was one of disbelief. The tall man was struggling to get the pistol out of his belt – Sam threw his knife with all his strength, the blade went in to the hilt and blood spurted from the man's neck. The tall man reached for the knife to withdraw it but collapsed dead before he could touch the handle.

"Well, that was impressive boy, but now I'm going to have to kill you." This was the bearded man who had been knocked down by Sam's kicking legs. He was still bent over some, trying to get back his breath. He showed Sam the kitchen butcher knife that he had been cutting cheese with. Sam struck like a viper, kicking the man in the throat. Down he went with a ruptured windpipe, dropping the knife. Sam looked down at the dying man, his breathing gurgling, while attempting to breathe one last time. Sam did not give the man the opportunity to breathe again - he picked up the kitchen knife and slit the man's throat.

Oh, everyone was glad that Sam had brought justice to Reverend Henry, but they were now wary of Sam. The men had escaped from the confederate prison of war camp during the storm. They had been the worst sort, but what Sam had done left the town people unsure of him. Everyone looked at him differently now – he was no longer the poor, cute little boy that had been rescued from the savages. Now, most of them looked at Sam warily with the realization that he was a bomb waiting to go off. Sam had gone through the motions of the funeral but he had already said goodbye to his friend while waiting for the town constable to investigate.

He rode east for five days through New York, Ohio, Kentucky, and then into Tennessee. He walked his horse up to an encampment of Union Soldiers that he had picked at random. After the corporal of the guard had stopped him, he turned over the boy to one of the officers. "Why are you here, boy?" the man queried.

"I'm here to join up," Sam told him simply – and that was that. The next day Sam became a Soldier in General Grant's Army.

****

Three days had passed on the trail with no sign of the Apache in pursuit. This made both Sam and Jock nervous, but made Beth and Big MacPherson happy. Dust and the sun had taken its toll, on both the men and animals. Each night camp was another alignment of the wagons to form a fortress. Twice against the river and another night alongside a rock butte.

Beth noticed that the small band had divided into two distinct groups; the first made up of herself, Sam, Jock and Big MacPherson, and the others with Sergeant Von Chek. She wondered if it was the natural division of leaders and followers or was it something else.

She also thought about Jock. She had come to know him even better during the past few days. She had decided that she really liked the man. She could not understand it; he was rough, unkempt, and certainly had poor English speech skills. The poor English initially made her think the man was unintelligent, but after getting to know him she realized that the speech was just a vogue way of expressing himself. After all he had been a mountain man. Finally, she realized that he reminded her of her father – not in speech, or manner, or even looks; but Jock was a man of shrewd wisdom - like her father. In fact, her father would always surround himself with men of Jocks character- fiercely independent, opinionated, and competent.

She remembered her father talking about scouts. He said they were different; civilians, who could quit - but did not. They did the risky business of gathering intelligence. If they lacked in other areas of Army discipline it could be overlooked, because they routinely took greater risks.

After dinner she walked out into the night to do her business. She was startled to see Jock standing quietly waiting for her. "You're not really following me, are you?"

"Sorry Missy," Jock was a little embarrassed. "It just ain't safe out here." He pointed out to the far horizon. "Me or the Kid always are keepin an eye out for you. An remember I'ma still workin' for the army. Wouldn't do for me to let the General's daughter get bothered by some critter or injun."

"I suppose when you put it that

way, it is understandable." She smiled at the old man and took his arm. "I was just starting to relax, because I thought you and Sam had relaxed."

"Can't relax out here. Been getten a bad feelin' all day. Think the Kid gots the same feeling."

"He never said a word." Beth responded.

"He wouldn't."

They had walked up the path towards the wagons; she stopped and looked out. "It's beautiful but forbidding. So tell me how did you come to live in the west?"

"Dn't knowed - I came to hunt and be'd what is now called a mountain man. Came west in sixteen, after the British fight in New Orleans. I was just a boy at that battle, but I done my share of shootin'. Fellow called Red Beard O'Malley was a trapper who brung me along and taught me to trap. Oh, those were the days!"

"You make it sound like such an adventure."

"Yes, guess you'd see it that way - lookin' back ya it was an adventure, but it was a lot of hard work and its lonely being up in the mountains all winter. Been snowed in from November to March one time. It was also dangerous what with Indjuns and Grizzly Bears; and whatever else that looks at your carcass as a next meal. Also, if you get hurt all alone there is no help. Many a man went off into the mountains and never came back. Hell, one of my many partners one time was checking a trap line an slipped and busted his leg. Set it himself and crawled three days back to our cabin."

"Well, that takes off the shine of adventure," she quipped.

Jock started laughing out loud. Beth followed his example and laughed too, in spite of herself. The girl was good people Jock thought.

****

Tatsahdago had been watching for hours; he had moved in quietly when the girl had gone out alone, looking for a quick kill or capture, but had stayed still once the old man in buckskins had followed. He waited silently in the same place until darkness had overtaken the camp and all had bedded down. Only then did he continue to move in the night using all the skills he possessed.

At last, he was only a few feet from the sentry. The man was a poor sentry, he failed to keep his eyes looking into the night. The man fumbled and rustled – Tatsahdago could smell the tobacco, now was not the time. He moved, then he could see the camp. The ghost was sleeping by the woman – her smell was strong. He watched carefully. Finally he located the man in buckskin, another warrior for sure.

He heard the match strike as the sentry lit his tobacco. The smell wafted over him, Tatsahdago drew in the scent of the tobacco; he liked tobacco. Moving carefully he came up on the sentry – when he struck it was swift and decisive. There was no sound. He silently lowered the man back to the ground. He looked again at the men sleeping – something was wrong. The Ghost and Buckskin warrior were gone, no longer sleeping. Tatsahdago faded into the night, now was not the time.

To the Apache the term hunting meant hunting for deer. Deer was the main staple diet of the Apache. They hunted year around and it was the primary duty of men to hunt and provide meat for all. Before a hunt a man ate nothing that would cause him to give off a strong sent; then he would smear his body with animal fat or bone marrow to mask his scent. A skillful stalker had to be able to approach within a few feet from downwind to strike with an arrow. Even after the kill was made the skinning and butchering was also part of a practical ceremony.

Chapter Fifteen

As dawn broke Sam could hear the angry voices from the encampment. Sergeant Von Chek's voice carried over the ground to him. "Why wasn't I woke and informed," his voice was shrill and laced with contempt.

Jock's voice answered, "The man would be no less dead if you had been told at two or five. Anyway, Sam and myself were watching, no need for another to lose sleep."

"You're a scout, not a sentry." Von Chek's voice now elevated to shouting. "You willfully violated regulations by not having an Army sentry..."

"Enough," Big MacPherson interrupted. "Fighting among ourselves is not helping." "You think it's okay to travel?" Obviously talking to Jock now.

"Sure," Jock replied.

"Then let's get breakfast and we'll move out after Private Kennard is buried."

Now that it was light enough Sam started following the tracks of the Apache that had killed Private Kennard. He was tall for an Apache and the stalking technique was familiar. Sam tried to think where had he seen this before - it would come to him, he decided. He backtracked carefully trying to see if he had missed anything. At last, he was back at the body.

He squatted by the dead man's head, the smell was familiar. He knelt down and moved around the body carefully. Private Smith and Bender were approaching with a blanket and shovels. Sam motioned for them to wait at a distance. He had picked up a rock that was almost perfectly round, just about the size of a man's fist. He looked at the rock as he squatted by the dead Private Kennard's feet.

"What the hell are you two doing just standing there? I told you two to dig!" Sergeant Von Chek was shouting at the two privates.

"He wants us to wait," One answered.

"Wait! I give the orders around here, not some civilian."

Sam was done, so he stood and walked back towards the camp; he tossed the rock from hand to hand ignoring the irate Sergeant. But Von Chek was not through, "Just who do you think you are," he bellowed. "You can't be giving my men orders." Von Chek took two strides towards Sam, closing the distance and balling his fists. Sam did not wait for the man to get within striking distance; he wheeled suddenly and lunged using the rock to the bigger man's jaw. Von Chek was strong but the punch startled him – he had never been hit that hard before. It took long moments for him to refocus. Now he was really mad – blind mad with furry. Von Chek lunged at Sam, Sam side stepped, wheeled and kicked Von Chek in the belly. Von Chek went down with the wind knocked out of him. Sam paused momentarily ready to strike again, then realized Von Chek was done – it would be a while before Von Chek would be able to get his breath back.

"You know, one who leads, just does not give orders! A leader takes care of his men and treats them well. You might have to depend on one of those men to cover your back sometime. If you're too big of an ass, they might just let you down." Sam walked on waving to the two men. "Please treat Private Kennard well; he died honorably in the service of his country."

The two men just grinned and smiled at Sam. Smith the older one said, "Don't worry son, he was just like a little brother." They walked by Von Chek leaving him lay, and started digging next to the dead Private Kennard.

Jock was stirring beans into the pot and looked up as Sam approached, then looked down and started turning the bacon in the other pan. Sam noted that Beth was already eating. Jock asked,

"Hungry?"

Sam picked up the tin pan from the stack by the fire and held it out. Jock heaped beans and bacon in the pan. "Find anything out there?"

Sam finished his first bite and looked at Jock until he had his attention. "Tatsahdago."

Jock looked wide eyed. "You sure?"

Sam nodded. Big MacPherson had been standing by the wagon. "What does that mean?" he asked.

Jock turned to explain, "Tatsahdago is a big man among the Patch. In addition to being a Chief, he's also some kind of a Medicine Man. Most of the other Patches is fraid of him. This one had a woman back about five years ago, bunch of miners caught her..." he looked at Beth then back at Sam and Big MacPherson. "Well you know what they did. Would probably been better if they had killed her – anyway after she told her story to Tatsahdago he killed her anyway. Then hunted down all the miners. Don't need to tell you how they died, but it was slow. He's been a thorn in the Army's side ever since."

Sam had removed several long pieces of leather from his pouch and started wrapping and weaving the rock.

Big MacPherson looked at Sam, "You know this Apache?"

"Yes, he is Puma's brother. In fact I saved Tatsahdago's life once a long time ago." So Sam told the story of Tatsahdago in the snake pit and how the two brothers befriended him as a boy; all the while he kept working on the rock.

There was a lot of silence after Sam had finished talking.

Beth asked, "What are you doing?"

Jock answered, "War club"

Sam nodded and replied. "It is used to get another Apache's attention. Used for personal duals between warriors."

"You know, this is a real interesting situation. Had you not saved Tatsahdago then you probably would have been dead by now; and by saving Tatsahdago, then rescuing Beth; then killing his brother, you know, he has now sworn a blood vengeance. By God, kid, your dammed if you do - and your dammed if you don't!"

"The word is irony," said Beth. They all nodded agreement.

****

Sam fell right in with the ways of soldiers. He was surprised to find that he liked the discipline, regimentation, and occasional skirmish. He was a private when Vicksburg started and had already fought in a couple of battles, but he could see from the start that this was shaping up to be a huge thing. In the Apache way of thinking a single battle is often considered a war. Never before had Sam been exposed to the day in and day out fighting that made up a single campaign. Not just a battle, but a series of battles.

There was confusion, stupidity, and arrogance, but somehow despite this, there was order and purpose. Hard Times Arkansas was across the river from Vicksburg and the Union forces gathered there. Most of the Union troops from the north hated this area, the river was big, deep, muddy, and hard to get across. The Rebs heavily fortified any good landing on the

Vicksburg side. The Navy had tried repeatedly to attack landing points to secure a safe landing.

Night after night Sam watched as men died trying to take the same fortification. The situation was simple. In order to land, you had to cross about a hundred yards of mud flat – and that hundred yards had become a killing field since the Rebels had the high banks fortified. The Navy gunboat would come in and provide artillery support, but the cliffs were too high and the Reb positions were too well fortified.

"Captain", Sam interrupted the daily briefing. Captain Sims looked around and noticed Sam standing, waiting to be acknowledged.

Sergeant Major McGhee barked, "Shut up and sit down Jones."

Captain Sims motioned for Sam to remain standing, he knew Jones had been reported on several occasions to be a good fighter, but the man had never spoken before. "It's okay Sergeant Major, let the man speak."

Sam felt awkward but he proceeded, "Captain, I'd like

permission to go in about an hour
ahead of the attack. I think I
can take out the snipers and make
it possible for you to cross the
flats."

"We tried that five days ago
with Willis and his squad. Willis
was an old Indian fighter and had
lived with the Creeks. We lost
them all - what makes you think
you alone can succeed?"

"Creeks are not Apache. I was
trained by the best in one on one
fighting." Sam hoped he had made
his best argument.

Captain Sim's looked around
stroking his beard while thinking
- what did he know about Apache.
"What do you think, Sergeant Major
McGee?"

"Apache are the best fighting
bastards on the face of this
earth. This here Apache Kid
probably has the only chance
possible."

An hour later Sam dropped off
one of the Navy gunboats in the
dark and swam for the shore. The
water was warm and he came ashore
in the reeds of the bank. It only
took him about ten minutes to
locate the Reb encampment at the

base of the cliffs. The trail up was well worn and easy to navigate in the dark. He slipped right past the sentry posted at the top. Now it was just a matter of waiting. The attack would begin at dawn. The rebel sergeants started waking the troops at about four. Since the Union had attacked every day at the same time, it would be expected to start at dawn. Starting with the Naval gunfire. But today would be different. Sam had the Captain's watch which he opened and felt for the hands – almost time.

As the first sniper finished breakfast, he walked down to a position which he had been using for more than three weeks. First he broke down the big repeating rifle and cleaned it then reassemble it. Just as he finished he felt a slight brush of an insect against his cheek, as he brushed it away he had only a momentary realization as the knife pierced his heart and strong hands kept him from calling out.

Sam could hear the longboats of Union troops sliding in against the mud in the dark. The sentry that should have given the alarm was dead in the reeds of the river. For two hundred and forty men, they moved quietly. No shot was sounded as bayonets and cold steel took the Reb troops at the base. Sam went to work in earnest now and systematically killed more than a dozen. One was an Officer in the latrine. The rising moon was three quarters, giving an eerie glow to the foggy riverbank below, as the Union gunboats blasted high into the cliffs around Sam. The Rebs, as well as Sam, could see the Navy barges loading longboats for the daily assault. As far as the Rebs could tell everything was on schedule.

Rebs started moving down the trail to the base of the cliffs as soon as the gunfire stopped. Sam knew they would not like what they were going to find. As the longboats approached the Reb artillery opened up, blasting into the mud flats. Sam dropped into the artillery battery and pulled out both six shooters. Blam, Blam, Blam, - Sam fired in rapid succession killing all six men, with one gun in each hand the shots sounded as one. He attached a short fuse to the black powder storage barrels, and then walked into the mist waiting for the explosion.

The Rebs were waiting as the union men came up the cliff trail. But now, the difference was Sam was in a sniper stand picking off key points. Soon Sergeant Major McGee and all of his men came boiling over the top and into the Reb positions.

Six hours later Vicksburg surrendered to General Grant. Sam was a Sergeant after that day.

****

A day later they were approaching the mountain foothills that had to be crossed to get to Yuma. Jock had been scouting ahead and returned just before sundown. Big MacPherson had been riding near Sam and Beth so they pulled up as Jock approached.

"Lots of Patch sign," Jock reported. "We can't go in that pass. They is just waitin' for us. Seen seven and enough sign to account for twenty or more."

"From what you two have told me, that is a big raiding party." Big MacPherson cleared his throat then asked, "What do we do now?"

Sam had been thinking a lot during the past day. "I have an idea."

"Right now I need all the fresh ideas I can get." Big MacPherson replied.

So Sam outlined his plan. He talked fast for over five minutes, not giving anyone any chance to object or ask questions. Finally, he stopped and was quiet.

Jock looked at Sam "You know of any water up in them hills?"

"Sure, you're almost reading my mind," Sam replied. "There is only one close source for water other than the river."

Jock and Sam rode down towards the river. They pulled off into a dense thicket with Beth and went to work. Sam and Jock took out their extra clothes and it took only a few minutes for them to stuff the clothes with brush. Sam stripped off his shirt and buckskin jacket, since he really did not have a complete set of spare clothing. Jock cut poles and tied them together, then inserted them into the clothing. Rawhide thongs were used to tie the dummies to their horses. Sam swung up on Beth's horse and tied his hat to the dummy along with his shirt; then he reached down and snatched Jock's hat and tied it on the other.

When he swung back down next to Beth, She looked at Sam in a funny way. "This is not going to fool anyone." The concern was thick in her voice. A small tear ran down her cheek.

Sam brushed her cheek, "Don't worry, they will be at a distance and won't know the difference until it's too late."

Beth grabbed Sam and kissed him full on the lips. He was stunned, but kissed her back. She broke the embrace and kissed Jock on the cheek. "Jock, I want him back alive."

"Don't worry, we intend to come back. Up you go." Sam helped her up into the saddle.

Sam pulled on his buckskin jacket and tied a bandana across his forehead. Standing there in moccasins, bear chested except for his cut off jacket he looked every bit like an Apache, except for his cavalry pants. She noted the completed war club hanging from his side – it looked ominous.

Beth looked down at Sam. "I love you, Sam Jones." She kicked the horse forward leading the other two with the dummies back to the wagons.

"Women, go figure." Jock chuckled as he pulled out his pistol and checked the loads, and then checked his Spencer rifle. "Well Kid, what do you suppose our chances are"?

"Fifty-fifty at best, probably less."

"This Tatsahdago, you reckon you can beat him?"

"Never have before. He's the best fighter I've ever known."

"This ought to be real interesting, cause you're the best I've ever seen."

None of the Apache tribes wove cloth. The Navajo, whom the Apache are thought to be somewhat related, are believed to have learned the skill from the pueblo dwellers sometime after 1680. A skill they did not pass on to the Apache. So most Apache clothing was buckskin. The Apache liked cloth, but most was acquired during raids. Apache women did not start dressing in colorful dresses until after the reservation days when they had access to cloth.

Chapter Sixteen

Sam and Jock were running on foot and had been running for over an hour when Jock laid his hand on Sam's shoulder to pull up, "Easy Kid," Jock said softly near Sam's ear. "I arn't as game as I once was."

They had just finished running over an area of very hard surface leaving no tracks. Sam was sure they would be looking for horses, not men on foot. Both men scanned the horizon then the areas between. Sam knelt and sipped from his water bag, then offered a drink to Jock. Jock took only a small sip also. Each knew that water could make the difference.

"We've come most of the way already," Jock observed.

"The low hills over there," Sam pointed. "That's where they will go to water."

Suddenly Sam placed his arm on Jock and pushed the man down. Jock took the gentle hint and went flat on his belly and held still. Sam whispered, "Stay, I'll be back." Jock watched Sam move, in four steps he was out of sight. Jock was a patient man so he waited he knew that the younger man was more agile.

Sam crawled and then waited, finally Tatsahdago walked into plain sigh, his heart leaped as he also recognized the other Apache with him.

****

Tatsahdago was standing next to his Apache father Laglo. He pointed to the area below, "That is where the blue soldiers will camp. We will be there already and then we will be victorious."

"You have many victories, but none with this Ghost. It's best to go home now."

Tatsahdago snorted, "Old man, keep your place. You no longer command and cannot. Just watch."

Laglo walked away Tatsahdago was driven by hate alone. There was no reasoning with him anymore.

****

When Sam rejoined Jock, he told him the bad news. The Apache had arrived before them. Their plan was to be at the water hole before the Apache and surprise them – Sam wanted to ambush Tatsahdago. Now that plan was gone.

"So what now," Jock asked in a whisper.

"I guess it's time for the direct approach."

"What you gonna do?"

"Just walk in and challenge Tatsahdago. You with me?"

"I'd rather go in a cave and get between a she grizzly and her cubs!" It was obvious from his tone of voice that the older man disapproved.

"You can stay and watch, but this has got to end."

With that Sam stood and walked forward. The group of Apache's saw him instantly. Jock had taken a couple of steps to catch up but was now right beside him walking ramrod straight. "I thought you were going to watch?"

"Eyes ain't what they was – gotta get closer to get a good view."

Sam smiled his thanks to the old man. They walked up to the group acting just as if they had been invited to Sunday dinner.

Tatsahdago was a bigger man than Sam by several inches and probably outweighed Sam by 20 pounds. Tatsahdago was all muscle. Tatsahdago had a Spencer breach loading rifle, a war club on his side, and a knife. Sam was not surprised that up close Tatsahdago appeared to be a formidable opponent.

Tatsahdago looked at Sam – eyes wide with recognition. He spoke in Apache, "So the ghost is only a lost one. You killed Prumi; for that you must die."

Sam ignored the man intentionally, then spoke in Apache also. "Laglo my father I have returned."

****

Sam Jones had been promoted to the rank of First Sergeant after the battle of the Wilderness. But the real battle that sickened him was Cold Harbor. The Rebs had scored a victory, much like General Jackson had done at New Orleans. They had dug in behind log emplacements, and then had proceeded to cut the advancing Union Soldiers to shreds. Even in loss Sam managed to become successful even as the army was enveloped in a misery of rain and darkness.

He had slipped behind enemy lines and had ridden halfway to Richmond. He had camped in a cold rain just off a road. In the early morning hours, a lone rider had approached. Sam watched as the man dismounted and went into the field next to the road and started pulling turnips out. Sam moved like an Apache still across the road and up next to the fence near the Reb's horse. When the Reb came back to his horse, Sam took him quietly and killed him with his knife.

Sam was right; the man was a courier carrying a pouch. It took only a few minutes to load the man with his turnips on his horse. He led the horse and body deep into the woods where he stripped the man and buried him. The pouch was priceless. Letters from President Jefferson Davis to General Lee - the south could not continue to supply Lee's Army. Sam knew General Grant needed this vital information.

It took Sam two nights to cover the distance back to General Grant's headquarters. Sam had dismounted and had walked, leading his horse through the Reb lines. They were so widely dispersed that he was able to slip through. At headquarters he told the duty officer that he needed to see the General right away; the man was busy and just told him where to find Grant. When he arrived there was another battle in progress. Generals Grant, Meade, and another General who Sam did not know, along with five colonels were just sitting on their horses on a hill in plain view watching the battle below. As Sam rounded the bend, following a creek, he heard the Reb's in the bushes. Sam dismounted and took out his new Henry rifle. A Reb sniper was in the tree. Sam slipped in among them and killed two men on the ground then shot the sniper in the tree. The man fell with a scream warning General Grant and his staff on the hill.

Another man came at him screaming the rebel yell, Sam palmed his Colt revolver and shot the man. About that time a dozen Reb's tried to shoot Sam; but he dove for cover and then proceeded to crawl through the low brush. They came anyway despite the brush, they had their sights set on a General and since they could not have him, they intended to kill the man that had spoiled their plans.

Sam dove between two rocks and shots bounced all around him, fragments of rock cut his forehead. Two came out in the clearing - he fired twice and they went down. Another came through the rocks after him Sam shot him too. There was a rock fence ahead and Sam took cover. Shots were coming from every direction. They knew where he was and they intended to kill him. Sam fired his Henry until it was empty, then pulled his Colt revolver and continued firing at the moving men.

Two jumped the fence and landed on Sam. He shot one with his Colt but the next click of the chamber indicated his Colt was empty. The man made a fatal error. He smiled in victory as he reached in his boot and pulled out a knife, a ten inch long 'Arkansan toothpick'. He lunged forward but Sam moved like a snake and plunged his Bowie deep into the man's guts. There was a pause in the attack this gave Sam time to reload his Colt first, then his Henry. Again they came in a rush, now all together. Sam had nowhere to run so he fired systematically and methodically as more than twenty Reb's charged. Their Rebel screams did nothing to Sam, as he had learned long ago to block it out and shoot.

Only four of the group reached Sam; but his Henry was empty again. Sam was now the killing machine that his Apache captors had trained him to be. After the four went down before his Colt, he reloaded and continued to shoot, ensuring each man was dead.

He was reloading again when a voice reached him, "Jones. Sergeant Jones!"

"Yes Sir," Sam responded.

"Cease Fire." Sam recognized the voice of General Grant.

"Yes Sir."

Grant wrote in his journal that night. I witnessed a remarkable display by a single soldier today. A scout under my command, a Sergeant Jones, single handedly fought thirty-two men – the result was thirty-two dead enemy soldiers. First Sergeant Jones saved my staff and myself. Additionally, he brought me the best of news. Lee has problems with logistics and his supply lines have been cut, so finally the end is in sight. Sergeant Major Sam Jones is recommended for his valor, and I plan to award him the Medal of Honor tomorrow.

****

"Welcome my Son. You have become a great warrior." Laglo spoke.

Before Sam could reply, another Apache came from the side, lunging at Sam, who was standing directly in front of Laglo and Tatsahdago. Sam moved with smooth blinding motion, as he drew his six-gun and fired one shot without even taking his eyes from Tatsahdago. The

Apache fell dead at Sam's feet.

Tatsahdago called out, "Enough! This one is mine. He has killed my brother Puma."

Sam held locked eye contact with Tatsahdago. "Puma was killed for stealing my woman. It was personal. So this fight between you and me is for honor. This is a family matter."

"My medicine is strong," Tatsahdago stated. "You will die."

"Your medicine is not that strong - you have been unable to kill me and had to follow me half way to the water of salts. Since, you have been unable to catch me, I decided to come and fight for honor."

"Very well," Tatsahdago replied evenly. He pointed to the trousers that Sam wore. "Even though you have become an Anglo soldier, you were once one of the people. You will be given the honor to die like one of the people. I see you have made yourself a war club." Tatsahdago pulled out his knife, a wicked looking stiletto that he had obviously acquired from a previous battle. "Knives and war clubs are the proper weapon for a fight of honor. Are you ready?"

Sam nodded his head in agreement. He drew his bowie knife, which was a good four inches longer than Tatsahdago's knife. Tatsahdago grinned, "I have always wanted a great knife like that, now I will have one."

The other Apaches were gathering in a rough circle surrounding the combatants. They not only wanted to watch, but this was the way in a duel such as this. Sam slipped off his gun belt and handed it to Laglo. Tatsahdago walked slowly down the hill towards Sam, he tossed his rifle to one of the other Apache men. As he passed Jock he wheeled suddenly and plunged in his knife, right in under the ribs.

Jock was caught by surprise, he knew instantly that he was dead; he put on a mask of defiance and calmly spit in Tatsahdago's face with his last effort, and said; "I'll wait a few minutes, because I know you will be joining me shortly." He slumped over dead, held erect by Tatsahdago's knife. The big man withdrew his blade and watched Jock fall.

Sam stood still, this was not the moment, he could not afford to be angry or greave. Tatsahdago turned and advanced towards Sam, Jock's blood was still dripping from the knife. Sam crouched and waited. Tatsahdago parried and lunged forward Sam sidestepped and slashed downward cutting Tatsahdago's side, laying open a wound at least a foot long. He knew it wasn't deep enough to cause any real damage, but it would hurt Tatsahdago's pride to have the first wound inflicted.

Knives clashed again and again in the afternoon sun. They kicked and punched whenever possible. This was a fight between two superb individuals, both in condition and ability. The observers could only watch in awe - they watched for one to make a mistake or one to tire. That would be the difference. Most fights between professionals are over in a matter of minutes, but this battle continued for more than a half an hour, an elapse of time lost on the observers.

No rules and only survival to the victor, each man fought with a vengeance. Tatsahdago tried to throw dirt in Sam's face. Sam managed to turn his head and stomp on part of the bigger man's foot. Tatsahdago shoved Sam into a clump of cactus. In return, Sam shoved Tatsahdago into the sharp lava rock face. Tatsahdago tried to use his height and weight to his advantage to force Sam down. But, even as Sam went down he managed to inflict another slashing cut in Tatsahdago's side; and was able to get a hand on Tatsahdago, using his might to toss him a good ten feet. Tatsahdago was like a cat – almost landing on his feet, he then lunging forward knocking Sam's knife from his hand.

Tatsahdago now smelled blood; as he moved in for the kill. Sam backed up and was against a rock wall. When Tatsahdago came towards Sam, Sam dove forward and down and rolled kicking his feet directly into the bigger man's knees. Tatsahdago went down in severe pain. Sam kicked the Tatsahdago's knife from his hand.

Out came the war clubs. A whistling sound of the spinning clubs broke the silence. They clashed fighting with the clubs back and forth for five minutes or so. Then Sam broke Tatsahdago's club; but the big man forced Sam's arm back until he dropped his. Now they just slugged it out, each trying to strike crippling blows. Sam's cheek was laid open, bleeding profusely; but Sam had broken Tatsahdago's nose and had ripped off part of an ear which also caused him to bleed. Now with both men on the ground Sam managed to get on top and pummeled Tatsahdago with repeated blows to the face and ribs; he could feel his blows to the ribs were starting to take effect now - the area was soft. Tatsahdago managed to get a rock and struck Sam hard against the side of the head, knocking him off. Tatsahdago got up with the rock in his hand deciding to use it to finish the job. As he reared back to use both arms to drive the rock through Sam's head he got a stiff kick from below right in the belly - which resulted in driving out all the wind from the bigger man.

Now Sam moved quicker than the bigger man and leaped up and onto Tatsahdago's back. Sam's legs encircling Tatsahdago's waist continuing to crush the wind from his body - Sam's strong arms encircled Tatsahdago's neck and slowly crushed the neck and windpipe. Tatsahdago struggled and flopped back onto the ground trying to shake Sam from his back. His breathing became raspy and almost squeaks, he convulsed in death and vomited - Sam continued to apply pressure until he felt and heard the neck snap. He applied a little more pressure - until all evidence of life ceased. He stood and carried the body to the edge of a crevice and tossed in what had been Tatsahdago - his adopted brother.

Laglo extended his arm. "My son, you are welcome to come home."

Sam had picked up his knife and sheathed it; he took his Father's arm and grasped in the proper Apache fashion. "I thank you father, but as in the way of the Apache and the Anglos, I will go to be with my new wife's people."

Laglo smiled his approval and was gone. Sam did not have to look around to know all the Apaches were gone, as well as Tatsahdago's body. His gun belt lay on the ground where Laglo had stood.

****

When the wagons rolled up two hours later Sam had just finished burying Jock. Beth cried softly as Big MacPherson read from his Bible.

"You did not mark the grave with his name," Beth said softly in the wind.

Sam brushed back wisps of her hair. "This is the way he would have wanted it. Your name on a marker does not make a big man – the memories we carry in our heart are what count. Anyway, nothing would last in this country; as long as we remember him, part of him is still with us. That's all anyone can ask for."

THE END

Epilogue

Sam and Beth were married two weeks later. They settled on a small ranch in California on the edge of the desert and grew oranges. They had six children, three boys and three girls. All of their children went to college and thrived in the West. Sam taught each of his children about the Apache and to respect the Apache ways.

Sam became a pillar of the community and was a successful rancher. For a time he was a Sheriff. He studied law and was elected as a Judge in his later years.

One daughter married into a newspaper family and ran the paper after her husband died. Another daughter married a rancher and fought for women to have the right to vote. Another daughter became a professor at Stanford University.

His oldest son became a Senator. The youngest boy died in the Spanish American War, fighting in the Philippines. His middle son

attended West Point and graduated
with honors. He served honorably
in World War I - and came home as
a Brigadier General.

Sam and Beth lived to see the
twentieth century. Their story
was handed down and told by their
children, based on a journal their
mother Beth had written.